A RAINBOW
IN PARADISE

A RAINBOW
IN PARADISE

•

SUSAN AYLWORTH

AVALON BOOKS
NEW YORK

Romance   Thomas Bouregy   5/7/99   1047

PRINTED IN THE UNITED STATES OF AMERICA
ON ACID-FREE PAPER
BY HADDON CRAFTSMEN, BLOOMSBURG, PENNSYLVANIA

For Adam and Dana.
For Anthen Joel,
with love.

And always,
for Roger

Chapter One

Eden plucked a tissue from the box on the corner dressing table and delicately blotted her forehead, hoping her makeup wasn't running. She glanced at the kitchen clock, then took a deep breath. It was not yet 10:00, and already the July sun was turning the high desert into an oven.

Outside, people milled about in the shade of the dooryard sycamores, chatting and laughing while a piano and viola tuned in discordant harmony. Most of the citizens of Rainbow Rock, Arizona—not to mention three generations of McAllisters—were here today, creating a scene of happy chaos. "Almost ready?" someone called from the front room.

Eden opened the door to the master bedroom and looked to her lifelong friend. "Almost ready?" she asked, and Sarah happily nodded. Eden turned back out, passing the nod to Alexa McAllister, who waited at the door.

Alexa said, "Places everyone," and the din diminished.

1

Moments later, the music began, Pachelbel's "Canon in D." The crowd in the front yard stilled, taking their seats, and the summer air filled with magic.

Eden entered the bedroom where Sarah was still dressing. "Sure you're ready for this?" she asked.

"Positive." Sarah nodded. "I've never been so happy."

"I'm glad. You deserve it." Eden blinked back tears as she went to her dearest friend, clasping her in a warm hug. Certainly she had never seen Sarah look happier, or lovelier. The ivory satin of her simple gown made her warm complexion glow and the wreath of yellow rosebuds and baby's breath gave her the look of a redhaired Celtic queen.

"Check my sash before you go?" Sarah asked.

"Sure. Turn around." The sash was the one concession Sarah had made to lavishness. Its deep lavender blue matched the moiré taffeta of Eden's gown. "You're perfect," Eden said as she fluffed the bow.

"Then you'd better get started," Sarah said with a twinkle. "I've got a bridegroom waiting."

"Lucky you!" she said, then raised a hand in a gentle salute. "True blue," she said.

"Through and through," Sarah answered, raising her own hand in answer as both women blinked back tears. Their childhood pledge of friendship had never held more meaning than it did for both of them now.

Eden sniffled, flashed another smile at the bride, then picked up her bouquet and hurried into the living room. There she paused just long enough to give Wiley Richards, Sarah's father, a fond kiss on the cheek.

"Hey!" Wiley said, grinning warmly and grabbing for her hand, but she winked at him and moved on. As she reached the doorway, the musical cue changed, a bit of a Mozart concerto. The groom's party, including the minister, would be stepping up onto the porch from the other end about now, she knew. Then the music changed again, the "Wedding March," and Eden began her sedate procession onto the front porch of the McAllister family home, the home that would now be Sarah's.

Just before she stepped outside, she was struck by an odd sensation, a sense almost of . . . She hunted for a word, but couldn't think of anything that described her feeling. It was almost as if this happy change in Sarah's life signaled an important change for herself as well. *But how can that be?* she asked herself. Then, chalking it up to borrowed bridal jitters, she stepped out the front door.

"Here they come," the bridegroom whispered, his voice ripe with anticipation, and Logan turned toward the door. He fidgeted uneasily in the heat, adjusting his tie and patting once again the coat pocket that held the rings. He'd attended enough of these shindigs to know how things were supposed to go from here, but he still felt uncomfortable in his new role. He'd never been a member of the wedding before. He wouldn't have been in this one for anybody but Chris McAllister. Chris was the first *belagaana*, the first non-Navajo, he had ever called friend, and the only one to whom he owed this kind of loyalty. He looked up, expecting to see Chris's bride.

But the woman who came through the door wasn't the pretty, redhaired vet Chris was marrying. This woman was a fantasy, a raven-haired confection in lavender blue. Logan started with a shock of . . .

Recognition? How can that be? He didn't know this woman. Oh, he'd glimpsed her before, when Chris's sister-in-law had brought her in from the airport a couple of hours earlier, but he hadn't really seen her even then. He saw her now. He hardly saw anything else.

She floated toward him, the lavender taffeta drifting about her like soft blue clouds around the sun. Hair as black as a moonless night tumbled down her back in rich profusion. He'd never seen hair so black on a woman so fair. She looked up at him just then and beamed a welcoming smile.

Blue. As blue as the desert sky in midsummer, as blue as the treasured turquoise. He'd never seen eyes so blue, especially not smiling at him. He shivered. It was the Fourth of July and hot enough to bake cookies on the floorboards, but he shivered when she looked at him. Then, as she neared, he caught her scent—warm and rich, earthy and achingly familiar. Logan swallowed hard and tried not to stare as she walked up beside him and stopped, almost close enough to touch. He longed to reach out just to touch her. Instead, he managed a stiff smile, swallowed again, and forced his eyes back to the doorway.

Eden trembled despite the summer heat. *Who's that?* she asked herself, barely able to avoid staring at the man next to Sarah's tall, blond cowboy. She tried to remember what Sarah had told her about the best man.

Best man. Talk about a perfect title! With the possible exception of the groom and his two handsome brothers, there wasn't a man in all of Rainbow Rock that fit the description better. She tried to think whether she knew one in Phoenix, or for that matter, whether she'd ever met *anyone* who better filled her qualifications for a ''best man.''

He was tall, better than six feet, and powerfully built. His hair was thick and black, fashionably short but long enough to show a hint of a wave over his broad, high forehead, and his eyes were nearly as black as his hair. Prominent cheekbones, a chiseled profile, and a deeply burnished tone to his complexion testified to his native ancestry. Then she remembered. Sarah had often spoken of a man called Logan Redhorse, an attorney for the Navajo nation who was Chris's best friend. She had extolled the man's stellar qualities, but without the faintest hint that he was designed to be a cover model. Either Sarah had been too lovestruck with Chris to notice another man, or she was clearly holding out. This guy was *gorgeous!*

Eden risked another glance and found Logan watching her, flushed warm with embarrassment at being caught staring, then saw him smile in response. Whoa! Can he smile! She saw so much warmth and promise in that smile, almost as if . . . Her breath caught in her throat. She blinked her eyes, looking away to break the spell, then trembled again, wondering if her knees would hold out through the entire ceremony. Yet even when she looked at him again, she still had the odd sensation that somehow, she knew this man.

Or will *know him?* Her knees started to give way, and Reverend Phelps caught her elbow. ''Are you all right?'' he whispered.

Eden forced a smile, nodding at him as she steadied herself. ''It's the heat,'' she whispered. The audience stood, and Eden turned her eyes toward the door where Sarah was entering on her father's arm, her heart still in her throat. Sternly, she reminded herself to remember the moment. She was here for Sarah's wedding, after all, not for . . .

Again she tried to identify the odd sensation that floated about her, almost as if it had come to sweep her away. There wasn't a term for it—not one she was ready to accept, anyway—yet the word *destiny* echoed in her head as she watched Sarah prepare to take her vows.

"May I have the rings?" the minister asked as planned, and Logan managed to deliver them both without fumbling or dropping anything. That surprised him. He'd been so busy trying not to stare at the woman beside Sarah, or drown in her sweet fragrance, that he'd almost lost track of where they were in the ceremony.

Somewhere in the background, the minister's voice was talking about the symbolism of a circle that has no beginning and no end. Logan knew circles. The People knew circles. Even their traditional homes were built in the pattern of the circle, finding harmony in the shape of the natural world. One day his people would build a ceremonial hogan for him and then there'd be another wedding, a different kind of wedding, an *'iigeh*.

With a start, he realized that the time must be coming soon. He was older than his *belagaana* friend, almost twenty-nine now. His father's friends from various clans had almost given up on introducing their eligible daughters and nieces. Perhaps it was time he gave the matter some thought. He had always known *how* he would be married—in a new hogan with loomed rugs beneath his feet and a holy man of the People to offer him the sacred blue cornmeal and sprinkle precious pollen over him and his bride. All he didn't know was when—or who. He had often pictured her, a woman with a tangle of midnight black hair—

He broke the thought, staring wide-eyed at the woman on the other side of the bridal couple. She was incomparably lovely and the black hair fit his image, but she was *belagaana*—other, alien, not of the People. And yet she looked so . . . He paused, trying to identify the odd sensation that had been coursing through him since she had appeared, a vision in lavender blue. And then the word occurred to him. She looked *right,* so right.

Right? A belagaana *woman?* He was getting his signals crossed somewhere. He reined in his wayward thoughts long enough to watch as Chris presented a ring to his new bride.

Eden felt a small stab of envy as Chris removed Sarah's custom-made circlet of diamonds and amethysts, slipped on the band that marked their mutual commitment, then replaced the engagement ring. Older than Sarah, Eden would be thirty in October. Here she was, watching Sarah take her second husband, while Eden herself had never married.

She paused just long enough to wonder why not. It was a familiar thought, one she had considered often lately. She'd had boyfriends, of course, even some who wanted to pursue the relationship, but she'd never known anyone who inspired her enough to make her want to take that long trip down the aisle, the one Sarah was making today. When well-meaning friends asked why she hadn't married, she usually answered with a quip about how tough it was to find good help these days.

With a twinge of guilt, she remembered one potential husband, a man she had really come to care about, who had accused her of deliberately distancing him. When he'd said it, she had known he was right, and she'd pondered that thought long enough to recognize that her own parents' rather odd relationship had made her leery of commitments. Then there was Sarah's first marriage—

She stopped that thought, unwilling to dwell on anything sad, not on this lovely day when Sarah was finally finding the happiness she deserved.

But if Sarah can find happiness, why can't I?

That odd sensation was back, striking at the pit of her stomach with a force so powerful, it almost knocked the wind out of her. She found her gaze turning slowly, inexorably, back to Logan. *Can he be—?*

No, of course not. The wedding bell blues must be getting to me, she told herself firmly, unable to stop herself from glancing his way again. He was looking at her, too, and the expression on his face suggested . . . But no. It was silly enough to have these ideas in the first place without persuading herself that he felt the same things. Still, there was something about the way he looked at her. . . .

You're acting like a giddy schoolgirl, Eden chided herself. She sighed and turned back to the wedding.

"Who's the dark *belagaana*?" Logan asked Chris, careful to keep his voice low, as they stood side by side in the receiving line.

"You mean the great-looking brunet?" Chris whispered, then, "Good evening, Mrs. Lawrence. Thanks for coming."

Logan nodded politely to three more guests, then murmured, "She's Sarah's friend, isn't she? The one she always talks about?"

"Eden," Chris supplied helpfully. "Eden Grant, from Phoenix. She and Sarah used to room together."

"Eden," he whispered thoughtfully. *Even her name speaks of paradise. . . .* Aloud, he said, "She's so . . ." Logan let the words trail away as he watched a beautiful, perfectly poised Eden greet an older couple, putting them at ease.

Chris grinned, obviously amused. "Yeah, she is, isn't she?"

Logan answered with a grimace, but he couldn't seem to

keep his gaze from turning back to the stunning woman with hair like a desert night and eyes the color of a summer sky. He found himself wondering if she'd noticed him, and what he could do to get her attention if she hadn't.

Eden, standing beside Sarah as the bride and groom received their guests, kept her voice low as she asked, "Don't tell me, let me guess. That's gotta be Logan Redhorse, right?"

"Oh," Sarah said, as if caught by surprise, "you mean Mr. Tall, Dark, and Handsome next to Chris? The one you keep staring at who can't seem to take his eyes off you?"

Eden made a face. "Yeah, that one."

"He *is* good-looking, isn't he?"

"And Phoenix gets warm in the summer," Eden answered coolly. "So why haven't you said anything, girl? You know you're only allowed to keep one at a time."

"I didn't know you'd be interested," Sarah answered in a whisper, then raised her voice as Mrs. Peterson took her hand. "Eden, you remember Mrs. Peterson, don't you?"

"The one who makes the prize-winning peach pies," Eden said, giving the woman her most ingratiating smile. When both Petersons had passed, she added with a touch of pique, "Why wouldn't I be interested?"

"He works for the Navajo nation," Sarah answered. "Lives out on the reservation."

"So?"

"I thought you'd become a big-city gal these days."

"Oh, you know me." Eden adopted a breezy tone. "I go where the men are."

"Yeah, right." Sarah didn't seem to be buying. "I've noticed that about you. And where are the dozens of men you're keeping dangling these days?"

Eden wrinkled her nose again. "Marriage has made you mean, girl."

Sarah chuckled in response.

"So honestly, why didn't you mention him?"

Sarah shrugged. "Logan hasn't been very interested in *belagaana* women—at least, not as a rule." She turned a speculative look toward the man in question, who seemed quite interested in one particular specimen.

The conversation was interrupted once more while Sarah, then Eden, greeted the Washburns and the Shelleys, then Eden whispered, "Logan has something against non-Navajo women?"

"His mother was *belagaana*," Sarah answered quietly. "She abandoned him as a newborn. He has never forgiven her for it, or the rest of us, either."

"Oh." Sarah's words struck Eden like a blow to the midsection. *Abandoned by his mother?* "That would be a tough one."

"I suppose it would," Sarah answered. "Logan's making progress, though—when it comes to women of other cultures, I mean. He really likes Kate."

"Who wouldn't?" Eden responded. "Kate's a dear. By the way, I've been meaning to ask you about her. Now that she's married your father and you've married her son, is she your stepmother or your mother-in-law?"

"Both, I suppose." Both women turned to look at the vivacious older woman who stood beside Sarah's father, her new husband, and near her son, who was now Sarah's husband. "She says I can just call her Kate."

"Works for me," Eden answered. "I can see why Logan, or anyone, would like her. I always have."

"She's a sweetheart," Sarah answered, "and Logan says he likes me, too. At least that's what he tells me all the time—that I'm not bad for a *belagaana*, that is—and I don't think Logan's the kind to say he likes someone if he doesn't.''

"No, I don't think so," Eden answered. "He looks like the honest type." Even as she spoke the words, she was struck by the irony that she had just been thinking about an impossible fantasy man who would always treat her with respect and honesty. With the moment of déjà vu came the otherworldly sense that more was happening here than met the eye.

"So, do you want an introduction?" Sarah asked.

"Not today. You have enough on your mind."

"Not too much to help my best friend meet Mr. Right."

"Mr. . . ." Eden shivered, unable to finish. "Maybe later," she whispered uneasily. Then she heard Sarah saying, "Mrs. Snow, you remember my friend, Eden."

Eden was determined to remember her purpose. "Hello, Mrs. Snow."

"Why hello, Ed . . ." The older woman furrowed her brow. "Are you well, dear? You're looking a bit pale."

Eden mustered a smile. "Yes, of course. I'm fine. I think it's just the heat."

"True, the heat is wilting everyone," Mrs. Snow answered, but as she turned away, apparently reassured, Eden thought, *This is weird. This is much too weird.*

The reception line had broken up and the dj, a family friend who had given his services as a wedding gift, announced the cake-cutting ceremony as "an ancient gesture symbolizing the couple's desire to nurture and provide for each other."

What a sweet thought, Eden pondered, *though I suspect it's really just an excuse to see which of them will try to embarrass the other more in public.* She shook her head, wondering when she'd become so cynical.

Chris delicately cut a small piece of wedding-frosted carrot cake, and navigated it with precision, carefully avoiding mussing Sarah's makeup. Sarah responded with equal care through most of Chris's bite, then stuffed the last bit into his mouth while their well-wishers applauded. The "Anniversary Waltz" began as both bride and groom attempted to chew, then swallow.

"Let's invite the bridal couple to start the first dance," the dj announced.

Eden applauded with the rest of the crowd as Chris led Sarah to the middle of the front lawn. He took his bride in his arms, then said, "Just a minute, sweetheart," and stepped up to the dj's podium. The wedding guests waited in suspense while Chris took the microphone. "We'll be happy to start this dance," he announced with a gleam, "but we'd like our maid of honor and best man to join us, please. Mom and Wiley, will you come up, too?"

Everyone applauded again and Eden cheered right along with them until she realized the crowd was opening around her, making an aisle between her and Logan Redhorse. That's when it hit her who the maid of honor and best man were, and what Chris had just asked them to do.

Feeling more than a little like the proverbial deer in the headlights, Eden watched the same realization cross Logan's face, then waited, stock-still, while he crossed the lawn toward her.

Dance with her, Logan thought as he moved across the grassy lawn, oblivious to the cheers of the watching crowd. *Touch her, hold her. Well, at least it will be a chance to find out if she's really just a flesh-and-blood woman and not some sort of apparition.* He stopped in front of her and held out his hand. "Dance?" he asked, barely able to choke out that much.

The woman seemed to be having trouble with words as well. Instead of speaking, she nodded her head and put her hand in his.

Warm! So warm! The energy that surged between them reminded Logan of the time he'd once grabbed an electric fence and taken the shock in his hands, only this time, instead of dropping the live wire, he longed to hold it closer.

She feels it, too! He heard her sharp intake of breath as she looked down at their clasped hands, her eyes wide with wonder, then into his face again. Unable to answer the unspoken question in her eyes, he gestured toward the lawn where Chris and Sarah already danced and their parents waited to join them. Eden nodded and Logan led the way.

Then somehow she was in his arms and they were moving to the music. *I'm holding paradise*, he thought as he steered her into an awkward waltz, wishing for the first time that he'd bothered to learn the old European ways of dancing. *She may be* belagaana, *but I'm holding paradise in my arms and I never want to let her go.*

"Lovely wedding, wasn't it?"

The words hadn't registered with Eden until she realized someone was directing them toward her. She looked up from where she was organizing wedding cake leftovers onto a tray and spotted Alexa McAllister, who had been folding chairs last time she looked. Eden smiled vacantly, then tried to focus on Alexa's words. "I'm sorry, Alexa. What did you say?"

"I said it was a lovely wedding," Chris's sister-in-law

repeated, a glimmer of amusement lighting her blond good looks.

"Yes, lovely," Eden answered.

It had been only a few minutes since the bride and groom had left together in Chris's road-worn pickup truck, tin cans rattling behind them, paper streamers dangling from most available surfaces. Eden had heard some of the relatives volunteering to help clean up and had offered a "me, too," starting at the table with the cake. Now, as she watched, Alexa began helping her, lifting pieces of cake onto the tray. "Reverend Phelps does a nice ceremony, doesn't he?"

I'd like to have him do mine and Logan's, Eden thought, then shuddered at the very idea. *What's the matter with me today?* "Yes," she said absently. "He does do a nice service."

Alexa worked quietly for a moment, carefully filling the tray with cake slices, then said, "When we've finished cleaning up here, a bunch of us are going into Holbrook for the Fourth of July picnic at the park. It'll be Jim and Meg and their little girl, Kurt and me, Logan, maybe a few of the other guests. We're hoping you'd like to join us."

Logan! Eden had barely heard the other names. "Yes, I think that would be fun," she said, trying to keep her voice calm.

"Good," Alexa answered. "We'll count on it, then." Moments later, the cake forgotten, she excused herself to return to the job of folding chairs.

Eden looked at her watch. *Almost five o'clock, and we've still hardly spoken to each other.* She and Logan had spent the entire day near each other, seldom farther than a couple of yards apart. The almost-electric power that surged between them whenever he came near had been pulsing like mad throughout the day, at levels high enough to exhaust her waning energy, yet they'd scarcely exchanged a dozen words. It seemed as if . . . as if they were both too overwhelmed to speak. At least, she knew she was.

I never imagined anything like this, she mused to herself, watching from the corner of her eye as Logan took aim at the beanbag toss, organized to benefit a local church day care. The smooth stretch of well-worked muscles beneath the crisp cotton of his white dress shirt reminded her that this was a man of confidence and power, a man she'd be wise to take seriously. *I've never imagined anyone like him,* she amended, her eyes alight.

The game ended with Logan winning a large stuffed animal and donating it back to the day care, then the other men went to join their wives and Logan turned toward her. The determined look on his face told Eden that Logan, too, had been thinking about their day together. "Eden, can we talk for a minute?"

I wonder. Do you think we can? "Sure," she said, nodding.

He took her elbow and led her aside, away from the tables where the McAllisters were preparing to eat the barbecue supper.

"Hey, you two! Where're you going?" Meg called.

"We'll be back," Logan answered over his shoulder.

"Give 'em a little privacy," Jim encouraged, while Chris's brothers and their wives chuckled in quiet assent.

"Just get back in time for the fireworks!" Meg hollered.

"Unless they're going to make some of their own," Kurt said, and Alexa shushed him with a muttered, "Kurt!"

"Ignore them," Logan whispered near Eden's ear. "Let's walk a ways."

"All right," she answered calmly, silently thinking that she'd walk all the way to Antarctica if Logan kept holding her.

He did hold her, his arm clasped warmly around her waist, leading the way around the baseball diamond and past the soccer fields until they were on the other side of the park. When they came to a bench, he finally let her go. "Have a seat," he offered, and Eden sat, looking toward him expectantly, wondering what he would have to say.

"I . . ." Logan looked as uneasy as she felt. He swallowed, attempted a reassuring smile, then sighed. "I don't know how to say this," he said, looking away.

Eden's heart fell. *Is he going to tell me to get lost? That hardly seems likely. We barely know each other.* Unable to think of words to cover their awkward silence, she simply waited.

"I'd like to see you again," Logan said simply, quickly, almost as if he had to blurt it out in order to get the courage to say it at all. "I don't know what it is I feel when I'm near you, but . . ." He stopped there, then said, "Tell me you feel it, too, Eden." His voice was very warm and hopeful.

"I do," Eden said, vaguely aware of the morning's vows echoing in the air around them. "I feel it, too."

He nodded, smiling contentedly. "I'm glad." He paused for a moment, then said, "Listen, Eden. I have appointments this evening, things I need to do. I'm not going to be able to stay for the fireworks."

Disappointment knifed through her. "I'm sorry to hear that."

He nodded. "So am I. When do you think you'll be coming back this way?"

"I'm not sure," she said, looking away. "I have a business in Phoenix . . ."

"The Old Woman's Shoe," Logan supplied helpfully. "I know. I asked Chris about it."

She felt her face warming. He had asked about her! "It's hard to get away very often."

"I understand," he said. "Eden, will you call me when you're coming back to town? Or at least tell Chris and Sarah to call me?"

She nodded. "Okay, and if you should get to Phoenix . . ."

"That doesn't happen often, but if it should . . ."

"Here," she said, giving him her business card.

"Thanks." He put it in his shirt pocket. "Well, let me walk you back to the others."

Again he led the way as they walked silently through the park.

"It's been a pleasure meeting you," Eden said when they had reached the picnic area. She felt the inadequacy of the words.

Logan grinned. It was that heart-stopping smile she had first seen on the porch this morning, the one that had given her such a sense of rightness. "The pleasure has been all mine," he said, then in a gesture Eden had only seen in movies, he stood, lifted both her hands to his lips, and tenderly kissed them. "I hope to see you again soon, Eden Grant," he said, then turned and strode away, leaving Eden to gaze after him with an audible sigh.

Whatever had happened between them today, she could only hope it would happen again—the sooner, the better.

Chapter Two

Eden pulled up behind the yellow school bus, waiting while it disgorged a half-dozen bedraggled teens in blue jeans, T-shirts, and plaid flannel. When it moved on, she passed, then turned on the gravel driveway that led to Rainbow Rock Farms. *I'd forgotten how early school starts around here*, she thought, *or how hot the weather still is the first week or two.*

In the few weeks since her last visit, the daily high temperatures had dropped by only a few degrees, but a shift in the direction of the afternoon breeze hinted at a turn in the weather. Within another month, they'd likely have their first snowfall.

The coming change of the seasons matched the inexplicable mood that had settled over Eden since her best friend's wedding. Perhaps it was the direction her life had taken lately that was causing her to feel so somber and wistful. She shook her head. More likely it was the directions everyone else's lives were taking while her own remained static, unchanged.

Even her father was moving forward. After eleven years of widowhood, he had finally remarried last winter. It was his decision to relocate to California with his new wife that had brought Eden home.

She pulled into the dooryard of the McAllister farm, then walked up the steps. Even the porch had changed since the wedding. Someone, probably Sarah, had hung swinging planters filled with bright red geraniums. Eden raised her hand to knock.

"So knock already!" Sarah threw open the door, then threw both arms around her. "Come on in. Oh, Eden, it's great to see you! Did you have a good trip?"

"Yes, great." She let her gaze roam over the changes in the place. "You've really been busy here, haven't you?"

"Some. Here, let me show you around."

For a time, the two visited while Sarah showed Eden through the old family farmhouse, emphasizing changes Chris had made since the home had become his own. Eden admired the way he had opened the parlor into the front room and dining area, and how he had remodeled the "mud porch" in the back to create a larger, more inviting extension off the kitchen. Sarah next showed her the expanded upstairs bath, then led her back downstairs to the master bedroom. "He finished this deck just before the wedding," Sarah said, showing off the bedroom's new addition. "He wanted to create a special place just for us."

Eden looked around at the comfortable, inviting room with its four-poster king bed and love seat. The intimate surroundings reminded her that she was an intruder here. "Look," she said, flashing a glance at her watch, "I know

Chris will be coming in for dinner before long, so I think I'll just be going n—''

"Don't be silly," Sarah cut her off. "I told Chris you were coming and he's looking forward to seeing you. In fact, we're both counting on having you stay for dinner."

Eden felt her face warm with embarrassment. "I guess . . ." she began again. "It's just . . ."

"I know. You don't have to say anything. You're remembering how it was with Jake."

An image flashed through Eden's mind—charming rodeo rider Jake McGill with his arm draped around Sarah's shoulders. If he hadn't gotten himself killed . . . Eden cut off the thought. "He was awfully possessive of your time," she answered lamely.

"Whenever he bothered to hang around," Sarah finished for her, but her tone changed as she said, "It isn't like that this time, Eden. Chris is wonderful. I never knew being married could be so great!"

"You're really happy then?" Eden pressed, needing to hear for herself what she hoped Sarah could tell her. She was one of the few who had seen past the facade of Sarah's first marriage to the somber reality beneath. What she saw there was part of what had kept her single these past ten years.

"I've never been happier," Sarah answered easily, and Eden could see that she meant it. "He's so good to me, Eden. It's not that he babies me. In fact, he pushes me to give my best to whatever I do, and he always wants the best for me. Then he does all kinds of little things to make me happy."

"Like what?" Eden ventured, then she blushed as she looked at their surroundings. "Or should I ask?"

"Like the wildflowers on the dining table," Sarah answered, leading her friend in that direction. "He picked those out near the hayfields this morning and brought them in at lunchtime. Or the wood. It won't be warm enough for a fire for some time yet, but he already has the wood box filled with stove-length pieces and the secondary box with split kindling. And there's more wood stacked outside, ready to go for the winter. He runs the vacuum for me— says it's a man's job—and almost always helps clean up after supper, and—"

Eden interrupted. "I get the feeling he likes being married."

Sarah nodded. "Um, so do I. Here, let's get some lemonade, then you can tell me more about what brings you to town."

They sat at the dining table, sipping from frosty glasses while Eden explained the years that had led up to the last few weeks. "I didn't know it," she said after a time, "but Mom's parents had put money down on the house we lived in and she made the monthly mortgage payments out of her paycheck. I guess she always resented that. Anyway, the house was in her name alone and when she died, she left it to Robbie and me, on the condition that Dad could live in it until he had us both raised. When Robbie turned eighteen last spring and graduated from high school, Dad realized he needed to make other plans. He'd just married Leona and she had relatives in southern California who wanted her to go to work for them. As a medical lab tech, Dad can work anywhere, so they picked up and moved to Anaheim, in Orange County."

"Are things working out for them there?" Sarah asked.

"As far as I know," Eden answered, her tone lighter than her mood. "And now I'm left with the job of cleaning out the old place, selling or storing or throwing away all the old keepsakes and junk nobody wanted to get rid of before, and putting the house on the market.''

Sarah's eyes lit up. ''You plan to stay awhile, then?''

''I initially planned to stay a week. You know, just clean the place up, get it listed, then skip back to Phoenix and let some real estate agent do the work of showing it and getting the papers signed.''

''But now?'' Sarah prompted.

Eden sighed. ''Having seen the place, I realize it's going to take at least two to three weeks to have it in decent shape. That's even if I hire out some of the work. I've got a full-size Dumpster coming tomorrow and I expect I'll fill that in no time, but after that there'll be painting and re-pairing some tile in the hall bathroom and I don't know what all. Dad really let the place go these last few years.''

Sarah nodded. ''I'd noticed some of the changes. But can you get away from work that long?''

''Realistically, I can get away for as long as I want. I've got good staff at the preschool and I've cross-trained every-body. We recently hired another teacher, expecting to in-crease our enrollment, but since we don't have the extra kids yet, we actually have more staff than we need. I just hate to be away very long. It's like with any business, in that there are some decisions only the owner should make. Besides . . .'' She shrugged. ''I like to think I'm indispensable.''

''Hmm. Don't we all. So how long do you think you'll be around?''

''Probably close to a month. Maybe more.'' Eden sipped her drink. ''Why? You have something in mind?''

''I just thought you might like some entertainment while you're in town. Maybe someone tall, dark, and hands—''

''Oh, no you don't!'' Eden had forearmed herself against

a hard sell. She had promised herself to stay cool and collected, to meet with Logan—assuming he still wanted to see her—and see what would happen, not anticipating anything beyond the moment. "I know how you newlyweds can be. You're like fanatics. Having finally seen the light, you want to push everybody else to do the same."

Sarah grinned. "Can't blame me for trying. Besides, it's working for other friends of ours. We have another wedding coming up in a couple of weeks."

"Oh yes? Whose?"

"Chris's sister-in-law has a brother named Max who came for a visit this summer and started dating someone local. They just announced their plans to marry on the Labor Day weekend. So you see, weddings are going on around here, and you could be next. If you find someone like I did—"

Eden laughed. "Someone like *you* did? How many McAllisters are there, anyway? And aren't they all married now?"

Sarah nodded. "You're right, of course. I got the last of the McAllister men, and in my personal opinion, I got the best of the lot. But that doesn't mean all the good men are gone. I kind of thought maybe you and Logan—"

"Stop right there." Many nights over the past two months, Eden's sleep had been haunted by Chris's attractive best man. She smiled, letting a glimmer of anticipation show through. "So, did you call him?"

"Of course I did! I saw the way you two were looking at each other at the wedding. Anyone who didn't know better might have thought *you* were the bride and groom."

"Really." Eden laced the comment with friendly sarcasm. "I'm surprised you noticed anything but your own groom. You seemed pretty far gone to me."

Sarah conceded, "You're right. I was pretty far gone. But that doesn't mean I couldn't see what was happening right before my face. There was enough electricity flying between you two to light up all of Rainbow Rock—and most of the Four Corners! And I'm not the only one who noticed, either, so don't even bother with denials."

Eden remembered the jolting power of the attraction. Even now it was almost enough to take her breath away. "Okay, I'm not denying it, but I'm not sure about pursuing it, either. There is Logan's notorious attitude toward *belagaanas*, especially women."

"Didn't he dance with you at the reception?"

"It was a courtesy," Eden answered. "Basic wedding etiquette. The best man is supposed to dance with the maid of honor."

"Over and over again?"

Eden shrugged. "I don't think either of us knew anyone else."

"And what about the picnic? Meg and Alexa said you two went into Holbrook together to the Fourth of July picnic."

"With a group, Sarah. It wasn't like we were on a date or anything. There were other people there."

"You mean other couples," a deep voice intruded. The women looked up as Chris entered through the back porch, pausing to wipe his feet. "Hi, Eden," he added as he walked into the dining room. He came around the table to give her a quick hug, then paused at Sarah's chair, standing behind her for a moment, rubbing her shoulders, dropping a kiss on her hair. Then grabbing a glass, he poured himself a lemonade and straddled a chair, plunking down beside them. "I heard about the picnic, too," he added needlessly, "and the way you two walked off together."

Eden, already embarrassed to know Chris had heard her comment, tempered her tone. "I was explaining to Sarah that there's no point in trying to set me up with Lo—"

"She didn't need to," Chris cut in. "I called him as soon as I heard you were in town. He's really looking forward to seeing you again."

Eden gasped. "You called him, too?"

"He'll be coming into town tomorrow evening. I thought we might go out to dinner together. You know, sort of a double date."

"He still wants to see me?"

Chris nodded. "He seemed quite eager. I'd say you made a fairly strong impression."

"He wanted to see *me*," she said again, clarifying the point. She had almost convinced herself that the power she had felt between them was her imagination—or at least, one-sided.

"He asked me to call him whenever you were in the area," Chris added, strengthening his point.

Eden gave him a searching look, narrowing her eyes. "You're not making this up as you go along?"

Chris laughed. "Not at all. I think Logan was really impressed with you, Eden. But then again . . ." He gave his wife a playful look. "What's not to like? Why, if I were single . . ."

"Watch yourself, McAllister." Sarah poked him in the ribs, drawing her brows together in an exaggerated frown, but Chris chuckled as he caught her elbow, then leaned forward to nuzzle Sarah's neck. The casual teasing showed Eden more than anything else how much warmth and respect the couple shared. If she'd had any doubts about Sarah's marriage, they instantly evaporated.

Withdrawing from her husband's embrace, Sarah asked,

"So how about tomorrow evening, Eden? Want to paint the town with Logan and Chris and me?"

Eden chuckled at the idea of painting tiny Rainbow Rock, but nodded anyway. It might be worth seeing what Logan had in mind. "Sure. Why not?"

"We'll count on it, then," Chris said. He pushed his chair away from the table. "What do we have for dinner, wife?"

Sarah answered sweetly, "Whatever you're cooking, husband," and Eden smiled, reassured to see her friend so comfortable and at ease. If Sarah could find happiness, maybe it wasn't too late for her, either.

Logan stood holding the telephone receiver in his hand, struggling again with the internal conflict that had occupied him for weeks, every time he thought of Eden—an event that occurred far too often for his peace of mind. The dilemma seemed unresolvable. *Why am I doing this?* he asked himself. *Because I want to, that's why*, he answered. *Isn't that reason enough?* Yes, he needed to begin thinking about marriage and no, Eden Grant was not a suitable candidate. That didn't mean he couldn't take her out to dinner, did it?

Petulantly, like a child defying a parental edict he considered unfair, he punched in the number Chris had given him. "Hello, Eden? It's Logan Redhorse," he said when she answered. Then he firmly told himself that the pause on the other end of the line did not disappoint him. *I shouldn't expect her to be happy to hear from me.*

"Logan?"

The warmth rushed through him. So he hadn't imagined it! Even now the power between them was just as real, even over the phone lines.

"Chris told me you were in town. He said you might like to go out with us tomorrow evening."

There was another slight hesitation. "I'd love to."

"Let's say I pick you up around six-thirty, then drive you out to the farm. That way Chris and Sarah won't have to worry about getting you home." He didn't add it would allow them to extend their time together, if they both wanted to—or cut it short, if that's the way the evening tended.

Again the brief pause. "That will be fine," she answered, and gave him her home address. He hung up a few minutes later, his spirits buoyed by the prospect of seeing the beautiful *belagaana* again. He calmed his conscience by telling himself there was nothing serious between them. *We're just two adults enjoying each other's company*, he told himself firmly, but he walked away from the telephone humming an old Navajo love song.

Eden changed her denim jumper for a pair of navy slacks, then decided against them and changed back. Studying her reflection in the bathroom's full-length mirror, she frowned in frustration. For someone who had had more first dates than any six women she knew, she certainly was having a hard time getting ready for this one.

So what do I wear to go to dinner with a man who . . . ? She stopped herself when she realized she had no clear way to finish her thought. Well, one thing was certain: there was no established dress code for this situation. She didn't even know what—if anything—was going on between herself and Logan Redhorse. Maybe if they spent enough time together, she'd find out. *Yes, maybe I'll just ask him.*

Eden cocked an eyebrow. Why not? After all, they weren't kids, and there was little need for them to play games. She made a mental note. That decided, she hung up both the jumper and the navy slacks and chose instead a pair of black leggings topped with a hot-pink tunic. Sarah had said to dress for comfort, and Eden always got compliments when she wore bright colors. She studied herself in the mirror again and decided she'd do.

She touched up her makeup and was just running a brush through her hair when she heard Logan's truck pull up outside. He was early. An unexpected tremor ran through her, and her hand shook so hard she nearly dropped the brush. She steadied herself with a long, calming breath, amazed by her case of nerves. Veteran though she was, she couldn't seem to help being rattled by this particular first date with this particular man.

"Hi," she said as she answered the door.

"Hi yourself," he answered, giving her outfit a quick once-over. "You look great."

Eden smiled. "Thanks. So do you." *Dumb thing to say*, she chided herself as she stood holding the door. The man looked *so* good, she was having trouble thinking. Had it not been for the feel of the wood under her hand, she might have stood there indefinitely, just staring at him. "Um, we're a little early for Chris and Sarah yet. Would you like to come in for a minute?"

"Yeah. Thanks." Logan stepped inside.

"This way." Eden showed him down the hall into the front room. "The place is a little cluttered just now . . ." she began.

"Sarah said you're getting ready to paint," he offered helpfully.

"Yes. There's a lot of work to be done before I can put the house on the market." She paused, stuck for words again, then picked up a stack of old newspapers from the couch. She planned to spread them over the carpet when she painted. "Here, have a seat. Can I get you a drink? I'm not sure what I have on hand, but—"

"Water is fine. Ice if you have it."

"Sure. I'll be right back." Eden grimaced as she left Logan sitting in the living room. *Great going, Grant. Stupefy the man with your scintillating conversation,* she reproved herself as she walked to the kitchen. She couldn't remember the last time she had felt so stiff and uncomfortable with a date.

Eden took a moment to prepare two glasses of ice water, adding a fresh lemon wedge to each, then placed them on a black lacquer serving tray, one of the few remaining treasures from her mother's long-ago reign in the kitchen. She added a pitcher for refills, then, starting down the hallway, vowed to have something interesting to say by the time she reached the living room, but found herself slowing her steps as she neared there, her mind still a blank. *Ask him about his work,* she advised herself. Experience had shown her that most men enjoyed discussing what they did for a living, whether she followed any of it or not.

"So," she began as she crossed the room and handed him the glass. "Chris tells me you do legal work for the Navajo nation."

"Thank you," he said, taking the glass, "but Chris gives my work more credit than I do. I represent the People— the Dineh—in several business enterprises, but very little of it is real legal work. Mostly I put my people in touch with other people, trying to get things done."

Eden smiled warmly. "That sounds worthwhile."

"You wouldn't think so if you saw what we do," Logan answered with a self-effacing shrug. *There's that smile again.* Eden caught her breath. *Think, girl, think!*

"Like what?" Eden asked, pleased that she sounded so calm.

Logan hesitated. "You really don't want to hear this stuff," he warned. "It's pretty boring."

Perversely, that declaration was enough to pique her interest. "Try me," she said. "What are you working on right now?"

His expression looked doubtful. "Goats."

"Goats?"

"Yeah. You know, *baaaa*. Goats."

He looked so adorable when he made that bleating noise that Eden chuckled. "Tell me about it."

So he did. Over the next few minutes, Eden learned that the Dineh had long been herders of sheep and goats—the sheep for both their meat and wool, and the goats largely as meat animals. "But the gene pools that fed our herds were primarily from dairy stock raised in Europe," Logan explained. "We didn't have any meat breeds. Lately, it's become a tribal priority to increase both the quality and quantity of protein available on the rez, especially to growing children, so we've begun a project to bring in goats that reproduce quickly and put on meat faster than other breeds." He interrupted himself with a shrug. "See? I told you this was boring."

"Not at all!" Eden answered, surprised to find that she really was interested. "Remember?" She refilled his water glass. "My best friend is a vet. Have you found goats like you describe?"

"Yeah," he answered, apparently pleased at her interest. "There's a couple in Canada who've been importing Boer goats from South Africa. They call them the first true meat breed. We've been working with them to build a herd here."

"Boer goats? Like the Boer War?"

"Exactly," he answered, and began telling her about them. By the time they left to pick up Chris and Sarah, Eden had learned that Boer nannies, properly called does, typically dropped triplets and quads in each birth, compared to other breeds which usually delivered twins or single births. Not confined to an annual fall breeding season, Boers were fertile year-round and, properly managed, could give birth three times in two years compared to the once-yearly births of other breeds. Their young developed rapidly as well.

"Do they need an exotic diet?" Eden asked, searching her memory for tidbits she'd picked up when she'd heard Sarah and her father talk livestock.

"That's the real beauty of the breed," Logan answered. "They do great on mesquite, sage, black brush—all native to the reservation desert lands."

"So," Eden said as they pulled up in Chris and Sarah's dooryard, "the Boers adapt easily to local conditions, produce almost twice as many young that grow nearly twice as fast, and yield close to half again as much meat as other goats."

"Exactly," Logan answered as he stopped his truck. "Here, let me get the door for you." Hopping out on his side, he came around the front to open her door.

With a start, Eden realized that a goat she'd never before heard of had helped them hurdle their conversation barrier. She smiled at the irony. The relative ease of the last few minutes gave her the courage to press a little. "I think I'd like to meet your goats," she said as Logan took her arm, helping her down from the truck. The touch, heated as an electrical jolt, brought them close enough to look directly into each other's eyes. Warmth and power surged between them, almost knocking her breath away.

Logan felt it, too; she could tell. He stood, studying her with a long, searching look. "I think I'd like to introduce them to you," he said after a moment. "They'd probably like to meet you, too—the goats, I mean."

"Goats, pigs, sheep . . . The man's a veritable walking encyclopedia when it comes to farm animals. Hi, Eden." Chris walked up beside them, Sarah at his side, and Eden realized they must have been waiting on the porch, camouflaged in the September twilight—and getting an earful about goats.

"Hi, Chris." Eden returned his light hug, then gave another to Sarah, glad the darkening sky hid her blush.

"So tell me. Has the Navajos' answer to Donald Trump been regaling you with stories of his latest business conquests? Or boring you with stuff about farm animals?" Chris asked, giving Logan an elbow.

"Aren't they the same thing?" Logan asked with a shrug.

"Don't you know?" Sarah teased him.

"They seem the same to me," Logan answered. "Everybody tells me I'm advising the tribe on business, then they set me up with goats and pigs." He shrugged. "Hey, how's a guy supposed to know?"

Sarah laughed easily, and Eden joined her. Any remaining discomfort vanished like bubbles on the summer air.

"What about Eden?" Chris asked as they finished their dinner and started toward Sarah's car. He was keeping his voice down, directing his words toward Logan alone while the women lingered behind them.

"Don't you worry about the pretty *belagaana*," Logan

answered, acting on the choice he'd made hours earlier. "I'll see her safely home."

Chris gave him a meaningful look. "You like her, don't you, buddy?"

Logan didn't dare say how much. He didn't even want to think it. He shrugged. "What's not to like?"

Chris laughed; he'd said the same thing himself. He measured his friend with a look, then gave him a playful shove. "Just watch how you treat this one, man. She's a lady through and through."

Logan's grin was slow and lazy. "Don't you think I've noticed?"

The women caught up with them and Chris suggested they all drive back to the farm, letting Logan take Eden home. Logan watched Eden's face, assessing her response. She met his eyes when she said, "I'd like that."

That was something else he liked about her—her directness. It had often offended him in other *belagaanas,* especially *belagaana* women. From childhood, Navajos were taught to defer to those who were older, and women were taught to defer to men. Navajo women seldom looked anyone but each other directly in the eye. That was how he'd been taught it should be. Yet it thrilled him when Eden met his gaze. There was nothing challenging or superior in her look when she did it, only honesty. She was what she seemed to be, and Logan liked that. He liked it very much.

He held the door for Eden while she entered the backseat of Sarah's car, sliding nearer the middle than the positioning of the seat belts encouraged. He got in on the other side and did the same so that they sat side by side as they drove along the road toward the farmhouse.

While Chris and Sarah kept up the light patter they had enjoyed through the evening meal, he and Eden sat quietly listening. He noticed her scent, warm and familiar, like the desert at night. He noticed her hands, lying loosely in her lap and, watching her face for permission, he lifted the closer one, cradling it in both of his. She smiled and leaned nearer, resting her head against his shoulder. It felt good there, as if it belonged. Maybe this whole thing was crazy—crazy and pointless—but it all felt good. Sometime early this evening, he'd decided to go with that, and deal with the consequences later.

He made quick work of saying good night to Chris and his lady, then ushered Eden into his pickup. She scooted into the middle seat belt and sat close beside him for the two- or three-mile ride back to her place. They chatted quietly, talking about the meal and the evening, Chris and Sarah, and goats. It still impressed him that she didn't mind talking about goats. In fact, she seemed genuinely interested in the project. Earlier that evening, when she had asked to see the goats, he had known there was something special about this *belagaana*, something worth discovering—if only for a while.

They reached her porch and he found himself hoping she'd ask him in. When she didn't, he reined in his disappointment. "Good night, Eden. I enjoyed the evening."

"So did I." She looked up at him in the glow of the front porchlight, her sky-blue eyes warm and direct and smiling at him, and he felt again that rush of power that always threatened to knock his breath away. Without pausing to examine it, he let it draw him, pulling his mouth down to meet hers.

She met him halfway, her mouth warm and sweet and giving. Logan felt the heat sweep through him. He felt her arms around his neck, her scent drifting about him, her softness crushed tightly against his chest, her sweet mouth yielding to his own. He was awash in sensation, drowning in it, and he didn't care whether he ever came up again.

When Eden broke the contact, he let her go reluctantly, then saw the heat in her face and knew she had been as profoundly moved by their kiss as he had. Her eyes glittered with an almost surreal light, and her cheeks flamed. She had never looked lovelier.

She gasped, catching her breath, and lifted a hand to smooth her hair, but did not quite meet his eyes as she said, "G-good night, Logan."

His own voice was equally husky when he answered, "I'll call you."

"Y-es," she stammered, "Yes, call," and stepped inside.

Chapter Three

Eden leaned into the kitchen floor's gray linoleum, attacking it with a vengeance. For three days now, she'd been mopping and cleaning and scrubbing with fiendish zeal, driving herself to exhaustion—and listening for the phone to ring. It had rung exactly five times. Once it was the plumber, telling her he couldn't get around to fixing her bathroom drain till the end of the week. Once was the glass company, making an appointment to measure for new window screens. The other three were all from Sarah, wondering if she'd had a good time the other evening and what she thought of Logan. What she *thought* was something she couldn't express even to herself, let alone to Sarah. What she *answered* was that he'd said he'd call.

I shouldn't let this happen, she cautioned herself. *I'm acting like a kid with her first crush. It isn't as if I've never dated a man before.* But just then the phone rang, and she ran to answer it, hoping it was Logan in spite of herself.

I never should have told her I'd call, Logan chided himself as he watched the goats clamber down from the truck. *I never should have taken her out last weekend.* He sighed and turned his attention back to the goats.

This was the second delivery of pregnant Boer does to the experimental station near Many Farms. The first group, representing two of the five North American bloodlines, had delivered their first young six months ago. They would soon be bred back, along with their female kids, to the two good bucks the Navajo nation had purchased at significant expense, each of which represented a different bloodline. The fifth line was arriving today in these eight does, all heavy with young, and in the one young buck that was now being led down the exit ramp. Five bloodlines weren't enough to ensure the genetic health of the species, but that was the best he could do until either the nation or its Canadian suppliers could import more lines from South Africa.

"Put them in there," he directed as his mentors had instructed him. The Canadian couple had warned him always to be careful to separate the new arrivals until he was certain of their good health. There was little point in letting a potentially ill animal contaminate the rest of their little flock, especially when these founders of their species came at such a dear price.

There they are, he thought as he watched them settle into the tight paddocks, *the First Man and First Woman of goats, the Adams and Eves of their kind.* Adam, Eve. Eden? He sighed. He hadn't had a thought in the last three days that hadn't come back to her somehow.

It had been foolhardy to spend the evening with her— wonderful and exciting, but definitely foolhardy. And it would be equally foolish to call her now when he knew nothing could come of the time they spent together. He was like a man on a self-imposed but unwanted fast who couldn't resist leaning through the door of the bakery, tempting himself with the sights and smells of all the delicacies he had sworn to avoid.

But don't you owe her something? his conscience niggled at him. *You said you'd call. What if she's waiting to hear from you?* He shook the thought away, recognizing it for what it was, merely another temptation, another way of rationalizing what he wanted—wanted so badly he could almost taste her on his lips—even though he knew it would be unwise.

But you said you'd call. That amounts to a promise, and you've always been a man of your word. He raised an eyebrow. That much was true. He had always been a truthful person; he'd even prided himself on his truthfulness. Well, that settled that. He had to call her. But what could he say? That he was just calling to explain why he hadn't called? That he was calling to tell her why he couldn't call her anymore? That didn't make a lot of sense. Still, he knew now that he had to call. His own honor demanded it. Didn't it? Logan shook his head as if the action might clear his fuzzy thinking.

"Do you have a phone here?" he asked Philbert, the young man who threw such energy and enthusiasm into managing the Boer herd, conscious of the role he might have in improving the future of his people.

"In the barn," Phil answered, pointing with his head, "if you gonna call local, that is."

"Long distance," Logan answered, "but I'll use my calling card."

"Guess that's okay then." Philbert nodded a firm assent

and Logan hid a smile. The kid's assertion of the small authority Logan himself had given was almost enough to distract him—just not for long.

I still don't know what I'm going to tell her, Logan thought as he walked toward the building. *Oh, well. Guess I'll decide that when I get her on the line.* The important thing, he told himself firmly, was that he'd decided to call. He knew when he thought of it that it had to be a right decision. It must be; experience told him only right choices felt this good. He walked toward the barn whistling softly.

It's probably the glass man again, Eden thought as she answered the phone, expecting disappointment.

"Eden?"

"Logan." Warmth and relief flooded through her. She felt melted to the floor. There was a long pause on the other end, and for a moment she wondered if she was mistaken.

"How have you been?" he asked.

"Fine. Just fine." She tried to remember whether she'd ever had such a stilted but highly charged phone conversation. The subtext was as rich as any she'd ever imagined, but their surface chat was as difficult as their first attempt in her living room. "How are the goats?"

Logan chuckled. She could almost hear his relief. "They're doing fine. We just got eight more does and a new buck in. I'm at the farm now."

That explains it, she thought. *He's just been busy.* At the same time, she was thanking the muses for giving her something to say. "You must have been very busy," she said aloud, creating an opening.

"Yes," he said, "but that's not why I didn't call."

"Oh?" Though Eden tried to keep her voice steady, she

felt the strength ebbing from her knees and leaned against the wall.

"I don't want to hurt you, Eden," Logan said, and she could hear him struggling with the words. "I think maybe it's better if we don't see each other anymore."

She swallowed, fighting the sting of rejection. "All right, if that's what you prefer. Logan, have I done something?"

"No! Not at all. You're . . . that is, you've been . . . It isn't you, Eden. It's just that I have other . . ." *How can I say this?* ". . . other commitments. . . ." He let the sentence trail off.

Eden closed her eyes and tried to choke down the lump that had instantly formed in her throat. "Chris didn't tell me you had someone," she said, hoping he wasn't about to confess to a secret engagement, or worse.

"I don't," he said quickly. "It isn't like that. It's just . . . *T'áá 'aaníí 'ádíshní,* but I'm making a mess of this." She heard him take a deep breath, then the next words poured out in a rush. "It's just that there's such a powerful attraction between us, and I didn't want to give you any false ideas, or . . ." He stopped. When he spoke again, his voice was filled with self-disgust. "I sound like a pompous jerk, don't I?" He snickered.

She laughed—brittle, nervous laughter. "Not at all. But I still don't understand. I mean, I understand that you don't want to see me anymore, and I guess that's really the only part I have to understand, but . . ." She paused. He could hear her dejection.

He felt wicked, vicious, and helpless to do anything about it. "Eden . . ."

She spoke hesitantly. "May I ask you something?"

"Sure." He gritted his teeth, bracing.

"If you'd decided not to see me, why did you take me out the other evening?"

She heard him sigh. "Because I wanted to. Because you are beautiful and I enjoy your company."

"Oh." The pause lengthened. "Logan?"

"Um."

"Why did you call me today?"

"Because I couldn't help myself." He waited a good three beats before more words tumbled out. "I'm sorry, Eden. I didn't mean to say that. Even though it's true, I didn't mean to say it."

She smiled, hearing the truth in his words, hearing something else, too. She let the silence linger for a moment before whispering. "I know what you're feeling." Suddenly the air was alive with the same buzzing energy she felt whenever he was near her.

Logan felt it, too; she knew he did. It hummed in his voice when he said, "Eden, do you think we can talk about this?"

"I thought we just had."

He heard her light tone, and he heard the way she was forcing it. He wanted to kick himself for the way he was making her feel. "I mean face-to-face. I'm driving into Holbrook tomorrow to pick up some things at the feed store. Is it all right if I drop by for a few minutes?"

"Tomorrow? You can get away on a Friday?"

"When the day is as open as tomorrow's schedule is, I can. So is it okay if I come by?"

She drew a long, slow breath. "Do you think that's a good idea?"

"Just to talk," he clarified.

She nodded, then realized he couldn't hear that. "All

right, but tell me when you're coming, or you'll likely find me grimy and spotted in paint.''

''I can't be sure when I'll get there,'' he said, ''but it doesn't matter to me if you're grimy and spotted. If you can indulge me for a few minutes, just for a talk—''

''Okay.'' She answered him quickly, and he had the feeling she had blurted it out before she thought better of it and changed her mind. ''Drop in whenever you're ready.''

''I'll see you tomorrow,'' he said, and hung up the phone.

Eden sat looking at the receiver in her hand, then finally set it in its cradle. *What just happened here?* After their kiss on the porch, she'd have sworn that Logan had been at least as profoundly affected by her as she had by him. Then today he had called her to tell her he couldn't see her anymore, and had ended by making a date for tomorrow? She walked away from the phone, as bewildered as she'd ever been, not even wanting to think about what tomorrow might bring.

Miles away in Many Farms, Logan sat looking at another telephone receiver. *I can't believe I just did that*, he thought, aghast. Had he really just called the most attractive woman he'd seen in years to tell her he couldn't see her again, blurted out that he couldn't see her anymore without so much as an attempt at explanation, then made a date to see her tomorrow? *Yep, Logan, that's exactly what you did.* He wondered if he was losing his mental faculties. He wondered if the People's doctors had a ceremony for the sickness that ailed him. He wondered how many ways he knew to say ''idiot'' in Navajo.

It wasn't fair to Eden, either. What must she think of him, hurting her when she'd done nothing to hurt him, then setting them both up for a repeat performance? He walked back toward Philbert, counting all the Navajo expressions he knew for a person of limited capacity and applying each to himself.

Philbert. As if he needed more guilt! With a jolt, he recalled he had promised Phil he could drive into Chinle tomorrow to pick up the very list of items he'd just used as an excuse to see Eden. Well, at least he could make good on that one. He'd give Phil the list and let him make the trip to Chinle early, then he'd drive into Holbrook anyhow. There were a few items in the hardware store he'd been thinking of picking up someday, whenever he could get around to it. His dad's old trailer would soon disintegrate under his feet if he didn't do some basic repairs. Maybe his foolishness over the pretty *belagaana* could serve a useful purpose after all.

Taking little comfort in the thought, he returned to give Phil the list and explain his plans to be away tomorrow.

Eden rubbed an itchy spot on her face with the back of her hand, fearful of smearing herself with paint or grime if she used her fingers. She cast a quick glance at her wristwatch; almost noon. The morning had disappeared in washing and spreading and masking. With half the day gone, she was finally ready to begin the serious work. A bead of sweat trickled down her face and dripped from her nose onto the lid of the paint bucket. It was going to be a long afternoon.

She sighed and took a break, sitting on the newspapers spread on her living-room floor and leaning back against the dry, fresh-scrubbed wall. The room was nearly empty now, most of the old furniture hauled away by the local thrift store, most of the accumulated trash loaded into the twenty-cubic-yard Dumpster which she had filled to over-flowing, then paid a half-dozen neighborhood boys to stomp down so she could fill it up again. She planned to paint the ceiling first, then the walls, and finally the wood-work. When all the paint had dried, she could clean the carpets and count one room done. Even the idea exhausted her.

She touched the rag on her head, making sure it fully covered her hair, hair she had washed sparkling clean that morning in preparation for Logan's arrival. Eden wondered: If she were a betting woman, would her money be on Lo-gan showing up? Or on him wimping out?

She smiled then, laughing at herself. Of all the words she had ever applied to Logan Redhorse—and she'd thought of all kinds in recent weeks—''wimp'' had never been one of them. *Face it, girl*, she told herself, *you hardly know the man, though heaven only knows how much you'd like to*. Some echo in her conscience assured her that, what-ever she didn't know, she wouldn't mind learning.

But dreaming of Logan Redhorse wasn't getting the room painted. Eden sighed and struggled stiffly to her feet. It was going to be a long day, and sitting here would only make it longer. Still, even as she turned her thoughts back to her appointed task, some longing in her heart reached out to him, begging him to keep his promise, to come to see her this one last time. She knew now that some unspo-ken ''commitment'' was making him reluctant to see her and that apparently there was nothing she could do about it. That didn't keep her from wanting to see Logan again, even if all she got from the experience was another memory to add to a small and rather exclusive collection. ''Come to me, Logan,'' she whispered aloud, willing him to feel her longing and match it with his own.

For the fourth time in the last ten minutes, Logan walked down the tool aisle in the hardware store, sure he must be looking for something. *Courage*, he told himself, *only I don't think they sell that here. Charm, maybe?* He'd definitely need something to make him welcome when he arrived at Eden's house.

What was he going to say to her, anyway? Could he possibly tell her the truth? *I can't marry you, Eden, but I can't resist being around you, so I thought I'd drop in for a little while just to bask in your presence and smell your hair, and maybe talk you into kissing me again before I ride off into the sunset. How's that sound?* It didn't sound so good to him. He couldn't imagine that it would to her, either, especially not on a day like the one she had planned.

Painting. Hey Redhorse, the lady is painting! Why hadn't he thought of that before? Passing up the plumber's helpers, he hurried to the paint aisle and picked up a couple of paint pads, a roller, a stir stick, two paper hats, and a package of brushes in assorted sizes. In his limited experience, he couldn't recall a single paint project where a pair of extra hands wasn't welcome. Pleased with his inspiration, he checked his watch, noticed it was almost one, then made plans for another stop along the way. He would *make* himself welcome. Maybe he could even earn a kiss, and not end up feeling like a heel for taking it. He smiled. Perhaps he wasn't such a *tl''id* after all.

When she heard the car door close outside, Eden stifled the impulse to run to the window. She'd been running to the window all morning and all it had gotten her so far was further behind in her work. Then she heard footsteps on the front walk and realized *this* car door was closing at her house. Hurrying into the front hallway, she slipped the rag from her hair, then used the front mirror and the brush she'd left near it to tidy up. Noticing the dirty blotch on her right cheek, she licked a finger and rubbed at the spot. The doorbell rang and she gave herself a quick inspection. What she saw wasn't great, but it would have to do. She opened the door.

"Hi," Logan said, holding up a brown bag from a Holbrook drive-through. "I brought lunch."

She hadn't thought of lunch, but now that the thought occurred to her mind, her stomach concurred. "That sounds great. Anybody who brings food is welcome here." She held the door for him, then noticed as he slipped past her that, good as he had looked in formal dress at the wedding or in dress slacks and a western shirt on their dinner date, he looked even better in snug blue jeans and a burgundy polo shirt, the heels of his boots clicking on the floor tiles of her front hallway. Eden swallowed a sigh and closed the door. "I've sent most of the old furniture away, but I still have the little table in the breakfast nook and a couple of chairs, and I made some lemonade this morning."

"Sounds good," Logan said. "This weather produces a mighty thirst."

"That's for sure." She led him into the kitchen where it took them only a few minutes to set up the lunch. Though he'd bought a burger and fries for himself, he offered her a breast-of-chicken sandwich and a side salad. "How'd you know?" she asked, then answered her own question. "You must have talked to Sarah."

"She told me you're a chicken fan," he admitted. "I wouldn't have known what to bring."

"Well, you couldn't have done better." The conversation lagged as they ate and Eden wondered what to say.

There was that "commitment" Logan had come here to talk about, but she wasn't in any hurry to bring up that subject. What else was there? She was just about to resort to the goats again when Logan finally spoke.

"I brought something else," he said, "besides the food, I mean." He held up the bag from the hardware store.

Eden shrugged. "What is it? I'm not good at guessing games. You may have to just show me." He opened the bag and poured out its contents. She gaped. "Paintbrushes?"

"I hope you don't mind if I stay awhile," he said.

She stared at the brushes, then answered simply, "Stay as long as you like." Maybe this afternoon wasn't destined to be so bad after all!

Logan stretched, reaching his brush full of dusty rose paint toward the ceiling. They'd finished the ceiling first. Then, for the past couple of hours, he had taken the high road, cutting along the edge of the white ceiling, then painting all the higher parts of the walls while Eden took the lower half. His height gave him the advantage there, and it was easier for her not to stretch so hard, or risk balancing on a chair.

He glanced toward her, hoping he hadn't offended her by taking off his shirt. He'd asked first, of course, and though she'd said it was all right, he noticed that she had colored a little and averted her eyes. Clearly she was as uncomfortable as he was. *I should have thought of a shirt*, he told himself as he finished the back wall.

Conversation hadn't exactly been sparkling. Perhaps they were both intimidated by the subject they knew they'd have to address sooner or later, or maybe, as he'd suspected from the beginning, they really had little in common—besides that electric rush that seemed to send sparks flying whenever they got within three feet, or spoke on the phone, or . . .

Logan stifled a sigh. He'd never experienced anything like the magnetic power of their mutual attraction. Now, if they could just learn to speak. So far their talk had been pretty much limited to ''Pass the paint'' and ''There's a spot,'' though she had thanked him several times for coming.

He smiled to himself. He was glad he had come. He was glad to spend some time near Eden, even if he wasn't going to be able to stay. Every once in a while he even got close enough to catch that fresh, clean scent that reminded him of a desert evening, and sometimes she flashed him a look of electric blue that hit him like a lightning bolt and sent tremors running all through him. Yes, it was worth a little hard labor to share a few more of those looks, a little more time just basking in her presence.

He set his jaw. The painful subject they couldn't avoid would come up sooner or later. For now, it was worth whatever it took just to smile and enjoy a few moments in paradise.

Eden sneaked another surreptitious glance at the attractive man working beside her. And it always embarrassed her when he looked her way and found her studying him. She never turned away without coloring.

To make matters worse, she could think of nothing to say to the man beyond ''Thanks for helping'' and ''Please pass the paint.'' She wondered why she was always so tongue-tied in his presence. Maybe she was just trying to avoid asking him what he had wanted to talk to her about, or maybe, as she'd suspected since the wedding, they really didn't have much more in common than the adrenaline rush that darted like lightning whenever they stood in the same room.

She shook her head. *It doesn't matter*, she told herself, coming to the realization she'd been working on for the last couple of hours. *It doesn't matter why he's here or what he has to say. For now, it's enough that he's here, working beside you, letting you watch him. Stop fussing about the future, Eden. Just relax and enjoy him.* It was such good advice, she decided to take it.

"I think that's it," Logan said. He put down his paint pad and stretched his stiff muscles, not noticing the breathless reaction he drew from the woman beside him.

Eden's mouth went dry and she swallowed hard before she spoke. "I think you're right," she answered huskily. With Logan's help, they'd finished the whole job, including the woodwork, in record time. "I can't thank you enough for coming."

"My pleasure," he answered, surprised to realize it was. "Let me help you clean up in here and put the paint away," he offered, "then maybe we can talk over dinner."

"Sure, that'll be fine."

They started by putting the paint away, carefully capping each can, then Logan went to a backyard faucet to wash clean all the pads, rollers, and brushes so they'd be ready to use again when Eden needed them. Meanwhile she gathered up paint-covered newspapers, stuffing them into trash bags. Before long they stood in a clean, freshly painted living room, admiring their handiwork.

"It looks great, Logan. Thanks again for all your help."

"You're welcome again," he answered easily, standing

near enough to catch her scent. Even mixed with the odor of paint, she still smelled delicious.

"Listen," she said, "about dinner. I don't have much in the house, but if you don't mind taking potluck, I think I can throw together a simple pasta dish and a green salad."

"I don't want you to feel you have to cook for me," he began. "You've worked hard all day. Let me take you out for something."

"That would hardly be fair, since lunch was your treat. Let me whip up something here. I insist."

He hadn't come here to argue with the lady. "In that case, pasta sounds great," he answered, "but I'm pretty dirty to sit down to a dinner. Do you have a place where I can clean up?"

She thought of the clogged bathroom drain. "I'm having some plumbing work done on the main bath," she answered. "If you don't mind using the shower off the bedroom?"

"No, that's fine," Logan answered, so she showed him down the hall to the room where she was sleeping, glad she'd made her bed and tidied up that morning. "The shower's right in here and clean towels are right over there."

"No problem," he answered, but the doorway was so narrow that their bodies touched as they brushed past each other. The brief contact left Eden nearly gasping.

Towel in hand, she fled from the bathroom—face flaming—then grabbed a clean cotton shirt from her closet on her way out and shut the bedroom door tightly behind her. She did a cursory job of washing up at the kitchen sink and changed into the clean shirt, then went about the business of starting water to boil, cutting up a salad, and regaining her waning composure. By the time Logan came out—crisply clean, smelling deliciously of fresh soap and healthy man—she had warmed some bottled spaghetti sauce, jazzed it up with a few things from her cupboards, and started the frozen ravioli boiling. "Dinner'll be ready soon," she said, barely trusting herself to look at him. "You can pour some ice water if you like."

Logan sat at the table and poured for each of them while Eden blanched the pasta and set the meal on the table. For a time, they ate quietly. Then Logan spoke, his tone casual. "Eden? I've been thinking about us."

She tried not to choke on her ravioli. "Is there an *us* to think about?"

"Sarah tells me your business is in Phoenix."

"Right. Day care. The Old Woman's Shoe. You knew that."

"Right," he agreed. "And you're going back there in a few weeks, as soon as you put this house on the market, right?"

"Right again."

"I've been wondering how you'd feel if we spent some time together for the next few weeks, just while you're in the area."

Eden just looked at him, wondering if she was hearing him correctly.

He stumbled over the next words. "I know, I'm the one who said maybe we shouldn't see each other—"

"I remember that part. You talked about some kind of commitment."

"Yes, but I'm not talking about any kind of commitments now, not between us, I mean. I'm talking about two grownups who enjoy each other's company just sharing some time together. No strings."

She licked her lips, put her fork down. Something in the

way he said it piqued her ire. "Did you think I had something else in mind?"

Now it was his face that darkened with embarrassment. "No, it isn't that. I just didn't want there to be any misunderstandings between us—"

"So, gentleman that you are, you decided to protect me by setting the record straight right from the start, is that it?"

He couldn't have missed her sarcasm. "Uh, something like that, I guess."

Eden was on a roll. "But you hesitate to spend time with me because of some other commitment you've made that you don't want to tell me about."

"I . . . I guess you could say that."

"And yet you want me to agree to spend time with you, anyway? No strings attached?"

He felt the heat in his face. She was holding up a mirror to him and what he saw shamed him. "Uh, well, yeah. I guess."

"Logan, do you think that's wise?" She wasn't being sarcastic anymore, or evenly viciously sardonic. He could tell from the intensity in her expression that she was absolutely serious, that in trying to avoid hurting her he had hurt her worse than he'd ever imagined.

Her searching honestly demanded no less from him. "I can't seem to be wise when I'm around you, Eden."

She made a sharp, high sound then, a quick burst that might have been a laugh or a sob. "And you still want to spend time around me?"

"More every time I'm with you."

She drew a long, slow breath while she studied her fingernails, picking at the paint that still speckled them. "It seems to me," she said after a while, "that we've come to a bit of an impasse."

They sat in the kitchen—Eden staring at her hands, Logan watching the floor. The kitchen wall clock sounded *thud, thud, thud*—each slow beat clicking off another second. There were many thuds before Logan spoke again.

"It seems to me," he said carefully, "that as long as we both understand it isn't going to go anywhere . . ." The sentence trailed away.

"You're setting ground rules," she said, getting his drift.

"I guess you can call it that."

"Ground rules," she repeated, as if adjusting to the thought. She looked up. "What you are telling me is . . ." She paused, coming to terms with all she had learned, piecing the bits together. "You have another commitment that will keep us from ever becoming serious about each other, so you want me to understand from the outset that you will never marry me and I shouldn't expect that, but you want to spend time with me while I'm here." She looked up. "Am I getting this so far?"

Logan had been listening, his eyes dropping as she spoke. "It sounds pretty awful when you boil it down like that," he said, "but yes, I guess that's what I'm trying to say."

"I didn't come up here looking for a husband," Eden began, and she saw Logan twitch as she said it. "But I think I might enjoy spending some time with you, too. What did you have in mind?"

"My time is fairly free just now with the goat project going so smoothly. Maybe I can help you out around here some weekdays and free you to take time off on evenings and weekends to spend with me, if you'd like."

"And when we're together? What will we do?"

"There are some things I'd like to show you out on the rez. We could make a day trip every now and then, maybe have an occasional picnic, just enjoy some time together before you have to go back to your life in Phoenix."

"That's it?" she asked, feeling a touch bemused.

He shrugged. "That's it."

"Logan, if that's all you had in mind, why has it been so difficult to say it? And why were you so sure we shouldn't see each other again?"

Because I'm afraid a few weeks in paradise will spoil me for the life I've always planned to live. Because I'm afraid of you, of the magical power you have over me. He dropped his eyes when he said, "I always seem to be tongue-tied around you, Eden."

She made another quick sound then, but this time he was almost sure it was a laugh. "Yes, I certainly know how that feels. I'm not exactly Miss Glib when I'm around you."

He smiled. "So I guess we'll spend lots of *quiet* time around each other. What do you think?"

This time Eden did laugh, then drew a deep breath. *It sounds like playing with fire in a dynamite factory. It just won't work.* "I think that sounds like fun."

"Great, then. Since tomorrow is Saturday, would you like to go up to Many Farms? Meet our goats?"

She smiled at that. "I'd love to, and thanks to your help, I'm ahead of schedule on the painting. Tomorrow sounds good."

"Can we start early? Say, six-thirty?"

That's inhumane! I'll have to be up at five! "Sure. I'll be ready."

He stood and crossed the distance that separated them, then laid his hand on her shoulder. The warmth of his touch shot through her, permeating right to the bottoms of her feet and the depths of her thoughts. "Eden, are you okay with this?"

She stood. *Okay? I'm confused and frustrated and a little hurt, but . . .* "Yes, I'm fine."

He held her by both shoulders. "I'm glad," Logan said, and the power between them whirled like a vortex, sucking all the air from the room. "I will enjoy spending some time with you."

"I'll enjoy it, too," she answered breathlessly. *Right up until I drive away from here and leave you.* She looked into his eyes, smiling a warm invitation.

The kiss, though expected, still caught her by surprise. She had rationalized that first kiss, assured herself it was only the newness of touching Logan that had moved her so deeply. She'd have bet money that she couldn't be moved like that again.

She'd have lost.

When he finally drew away, she clung to him, fearful that if he let her go, she might simply crumple to the floor. . . . "Logan?"

He took his hands away; she instantly felt the loss. "Yes?"

"You know I wouldn't ask you to stop if I didn't like it so much."

He smiled, a wry look. "I know," he said. "Me, too." He kissed his index finger, then placed it on the tip of her nose. "See you tomorrow."

She smiled back. "Right. Bright and early."

Chapter Four

Well, it's early, but I'll be darned if it's bright. Then again, neither am I. Eden almost grumbled aloud as she faced the bathroom mirror, cringing at the red eyes and bloated face that were reflected back at her. What with the incessant dreams of Logan and the hours of wakefulness mixed in, she hadn't had much of a night. Now it was going to take some fine alchemy to get herself into a condition that wouldn't send people running in panic if they looked at her, and to accomplish that before Logan got here? She looked at the clock on the bathroom wall, and groaned.

Carefully, lest she break something while still in this fragile-as-glass morning mood, she began to prepare. She had chosen blue jeans and a comfortable, striped ''big shirt'' with short sleeves. These she had laid out, together with a clean pair of cotton socks and her sneakers, on the chair beside the bed before she'd retired last night. In case the day grew cool or clouded over, she had selected a sweatshirt with the ASU Sun Devils logo. Then, because she was heading out onto the desert, she had packed a second pair of shoes, two extra pairs of socks, a canteen of water, and several small items she might need if she were stranded—toothbrush and toothpaste, a hairbrush, a small package of energy bars—into an old bookpack she had found in the closet of her former bedroom, left over from her high school days. The backpack and sweatshirt she now set in the hallway by the front door. Then she hurried to shower and scrub, brush and groom, eat a small breakfast, and make up her face.

Years of hurry-up practice paid off for her this morning, and she was feeling more or less put together by the time Logan knocked, not even so fragile anymore.

"Hi," he said as she opened the door.

"Hi yourself," she answered.

"Ready?"

"Ready." She picked up her sweatshirt and backpack, locked the front door behind her, tucking the key into the pack's outside pocket, and followed Logan to the truck.

"I apologize for the early hour," he offered as he held the door for her.

"No need," she said, silently congratulating herself that he probably couldn't even tell she was definitely not a morning person. "It's pretty out this morning, isn't it?"

"Umm," he answered. She assumed it was an affirmative. "We're seeing the White Dawn now."

"White Dawn?"

So he told her the story of how Changing Woman, the first woman that ever was, who bore all the human race, had married Sun and taken him to live with her in her hogan. Then, seeing that her sister, Turquoise Woman, who lived at the other side of the world, was alone and lonely,

Changing Woman had encouraged her husband to marry her sister as well. Every day, Sun made the journey across the sky from the home of Changing Woman to the home of his second wife.

"As he goes out," Logan finished, "he puts on his gray fox fur to protect him from the morning chill. Later, when he is farther on his journey and the day is warmer, he puts on a yellow fox fur and brings the Yellow Dawn."

"That's a charming story," Eden said, looking around her. "I think he's getting ready to change furs about now."

"Any moment now," Logan answered. "Look to the east. The color is beginning to spread."

It was indeed, the pale, pastel colors of White Dawn growing richer as the sun rose nearer the horizon, soft mauve warming to rich coral, buttery yellow melting into liquid golden light.

"Ah, there he is," Logan said as the sun crested the horizon. Then he began to speak, soft Navajo words that fell in a chanting pattern.

"What is that you're saying?" Eden asked.

"House made of pollen, house made of dawn, house made of morning light," Logan quoted, translating into English. "It's the beginning of a chant that Navajo children learn early."

"Like a prayer to the sun?"

"Something like that. It's part of a longer ceremony." He turned back to the road.

"Is it part of the Beautyway?" she asked.

Logan's eyes widened. "You know the Beautyway?"

"Oh, no! I don't pretend to know it. It takes days and days to perform it correctly, doesn't it?"

"Yes, many days," Logan agreed. "I guess I'm just surprised that you'd know anything about it all."

"I read a lot," Eden answered, "and I've been interested in the ceremonies that were native to this land ever since I was a little child."

"I'm impressed."

"So am I," she answered. "Some of the ceremonies are filled with fine poetry, beautiful lines."

"I always thought so."

For a while they traveled in silence. Then Eden shivered and pulled her sweatshirt up around her, exposing the university logo. "You went to ASU?" Logan asked her.

"Um-hm." She pointed at the mascot. "Just call me a Sun Devil."

"Me, too," he said.

"No kidding? When were you there?"

The conversation turned then to their memories of their college alma mater. Although Logan was a few months younger and had gone to the school in Tempe sometime after Eden had completed most of her general coursework, they had shared most of the same experiences, including the same professor for their introductory geology course, and one spectacular football win against rival University of Arizona that they'd both attended in the Sun Devils' stadium during Eden's last year and Logan's third.

"That's when I first started rooming with Chris," Logan told her. "He insisted on taking me to that game. I'd pretty much avoided the football stadium before then."

"Just too much studying?" Eden asked.

"That, too. Mostly I couldn't imagine being in the same place with sixty-five thousand other people, all at the same time."

Eden chuckled. "I guess that would be something of a change."

"Compared to this?" Logan gestured around them. They

had passed onto the reservation shortly after leaving Rainbow Rock, and they'd hardly seen another human being since then. There wasn't another human in sight as Eden looked, following Logan's gesture.

"You're right," she said. "It is a big change."

"Call it culture shock."

"But you managed."

He shrugged. "A lot of good people helped me. Most of the time I just wanted to duck my head and run—back to the rez, to my grandmother's hogan, to the life I'd known as a boy."

"So why didn't you?"

Logan shrugged. "I'm not always sure. Sometimes I tell myself I just didn't want to disappoint all the people who were counting on me, but when I'm most honest with myself, I think maybe I'm the one I didn't want to disappoint. Somehow I always knew my life and work would need to accommodate the larger world, the world outside the reservation. Many of us—that is, people in my generation and yours, and younger people, too—I must reach out to that world if the people are going to have a place in the future."

"You feel a very great loyalty to your people, don't you?"

"The greatest," he answered, and the look he gave Eden shook her, making her think suddenly of "commitments" that couldn't be spoken.

"They're adorable, Logan. Hey, stop it, you!" Eden laughed and pulled her shirttail away from the little black-and-white doe that suckled it as if she expected it to feed her. "Stop that!" she ordered, pushing the baby away, then bending to rub her head. "Oh, aren't you a sweetheart?"

For the past few minutes, Eden had been playing in the

small paddock that housed the goat kids from the last two births—all seven of them, the eldest only five days old. The kids, their heads only slightly higher than Eden's knees, had quickly captivated her with their antics. Logan had been content to sit watching, amused at her childlike wonder, amazed at her apparently unlimited capacity for joy. She laughed again as he watched, turning in a circle to shake away the young buck that was now chewing at the back of her shirt. Her tangle of black curls rippled like a banner on the wind and her laughter flowed over him like water from a desert spring. He felt that laughter clutching at a place near his heart, and knew he was in trouble.

"If you were a Navajo child, I would have to scold you," he said softly, his heart not in the mood for scolding.

"Me? Why?" she asked, her face bright with innocent delight.

"Navajo children always play with the young animals," he answered, "but they're always admonished to remember these goats are food."

He saw the shuttered look that came over her eyes as she took the shirt from the little goat's mouth and pushed out through the gate, closing it tightly behind her. "I guess I let myself forget," she said. "I'm sorry."

"No, *I'm* sorry," he answered, feeling like a heel for disrupting her moment of starry-eyed delight.

"Are you going to eat them all?"

"Well, probably not me personally, but that's why they're here."

Her color darkened. "I didn't mean you personally," she said. "I meant, won't you save any of these for breeding purposes?"

"Actually, yes, we will. Most of the little does, if they have the good characteristics we're looking for in the breed, will be bred back to one of the other lines, not those of their father or mother. That necessitates keeping excellent records on all these births, of course.''

"Of course. And the little bucks?'' She reached inside the pen to rub the ears of the one little buck that had tried to eat her shirttail.

"Only the very biggest and best of those will be saved,'' Logan answered, "and probably none from this batch.''

"Oh.'' Eden drew her hand away from the hungry little one.

"So, would you like to see the rest of the operation?''

"Sure,'' she answered, following him away from the baby goats.

Eden found the goat project a combination of hodgepodge makeshift, largely in the building materials, and meticulous crafting, particularly with regard to the way breeding records were kept on each of the animals. Every goat was marked with a tag in its right ear, the number on that tag corresponding to its place on an elaborate pedigree chart kept both on paper, in manual form, and on disk, in a computer terminal belonging to the Navajo nation and assigned to this project.

"We keep the manual backup system because we can never guarantee a steady power supply,'' Logan explained as Eden examined the records. "Then, every time the data in the pedigree files are altered, we send data files to the mainframe computer at the nation's headquarters in Window Rock, so there's another backup copy.''

"I'm impressed,'' Eden responded as she examined the pedigree files. "You have complete data on every goat in the project: when it was born and where, its parents and their parents and theirs. It looks like you have the ancestry on most of these goats back at least four generations.''

"Four is the minimum we'll accept here," Logan answered. "We have data back for eight generations on some of the younger goats, those in the lines that have been here longer."

"Wow," Eden answered. "Most humans don't know as much about their ancestry as you know about these goats' ancestors."

Logan shrugged. "Most humans are choosing their mates from an enormous gene pool. We have to be more careful with these goats, since we're breeding them back a couple of times a year, and we're working with only five bloodlines."

"Still, I think most people would be amazed if they knew this much about their own bloodlines."

"Among the *belagaana*, perhaps," Logan answered with a twinkle. "We Dineh have always prided ourselves on knowing where we come from."

"I've heard that," Eden answered. "It's what anthropologists call your consanguinity laws."

"Right," Logan said, "our way of knowing who is distantly or closely related to whom. In practice, it doesn't seem to mean much except when you are thinking about getting married and you need to consult the tribal elders to be sure the clans aren't too closely related. Or"—his eyes danced with mischief—"if you suddenly come into money and the People around you want to know whether they can claim blood relationship or not."

"So tell me about your people," Eden asked, fully aware that she was treading on unsteady ground should the subject of his mother come up.

"Among the Dineh, every individual is identified by his people. I am Logan Redhorse, born to the Tall House People, born for the Salt People."

"So those are your clans," she said, trying hard to remember what she knew of Navajo kinship laws, and the few clans she had heard of before.

"Yes," he said, "but only because my grandmother adopted me as her own son, giving me the same kinship as my father has—more like his brother than his child. You see, the Dineh inherit their clan affiliation through their mothers, and my natural mother was—"

"—*belagaana*," Eden finished for him. "Sarah told me."

He nodded. "I am born to the Tall House People, my grandmother's clan, because she claims me as her child. I am born *for* the Salt Clan—"

"—That would be your grandfather's family . . ."

"Yes, but again, it is borrowed inheritance, since I can't claim any right of inheritance from my mother, as other Dineh do. My grandmother has often told me that my mother was of the Surface-of-the-Earth people, those who walk upon the face of their Mother Earth without ever knowing her or belonging to her, as the People do."

"You are very close to your grandmother, aren't you?"

Again Logan shrugged. "Close or far, she's the one person who has always been in my life. I owe her a great deal."

Eden felt her throat tightening, but refused to give in too much. "I hope she appreciates what a fine man you've become," she said simply.

"She thinks I've become too like the *belagaana* I live among," he answered. "Well, how about a picnic? Would you like to see some of Canyon de Chelly?"

"I'd love to," Eden answered, ready to let the conversation take a different turn.

"All these years I lived within two hours' drive of this, and I never even knew it was here." Eden shook her head in wonder, amazed by everything she saw in the mystical reaches of Canyon de Chelly. She and Logan had passed through Chinle a little after 11:30. Now it was barely noon and already they were moving into a deep and widening gorge that dwarfed them with its sheer magnificence.

"Impressed?" Logan asked, apparently pleased.

"Astounded." Eden leaned down to get an angle on the truck's windshield. "How high are these walls, anyway?"

"I'm told they average about a thousand feet, though there are clear exceptions. In one place, the walls are more than seventeen hundred feet above the canyon floor." He drove toward them.

"Amazing," Eden said again, staring in wonder. "Walls" was the right name for the carved sides of this steep chasm. They appeared to have been chiseled from red and dun sandstone, then polished smooth. Striped with color, like the painted hills that had given Rainbow Rock and the Painted Desert their names, the layers of sandstone lay hundreds of feet thick, natural monuments that towered above the canyon's tiny occupants. "I can imagine how the old ones saw this place."

"It was the ancient heart of Dinehtah," Logan answered, using the Navajos' name for their traditional homeland.

Eden saw the look on his face and understood more than Logan was telling her in words; much of his own heart was here as well. "It's mystical," she answered. "In a place like this, one could almost believe in magic."

"Or faith, perhaps." Logan drove the truck off-road, heading toward one of the sheer rock walls that marked the canyon's boundary. "This canyon is considered sacred by the People, and within it, many places have specific meaning.''

''I'm not surprised,'' Eden answered, trying to sense the place's spirit. The canyon had a sacred feeling, like a giant natural cathedral, its ceiling open to the sky. ''There's a reverent feeling here, like in a holy place.''

''It has been that,'' Logan agreed. ''It's also been a formidable fortress. In the history of the Dineh, I expect this canyon has served one purpose at least as much as the other.''

''A fortress,'' Eden said thoughtfully, then looking about at the faces of sheer, forbidding rock, she nodded. ''I can see that, too. People who holed up within these walls could easily defend themselves against anyone trying to enter from Chinle.''

''It was actually much simpler than that,'' Logan said. He stopped the truck a few hundred yards from one looming stone wall, turned off the engine, then turned to speak, one arm on the back of the truck's seat. As his hand touched her shoulder, the inevitable power flowed between them, enlivening the small space within the pickup's cab. ''Often during the Navajo Wars, the people hid in the nooks and crannies along the canyon floor while warriors gathered on the heights, raining down stones and arrows on anyone who attempted to follow their innocent ones to their hiding places.''

Eden nodded. Encouraged, Logan toyed with a tendril of her dark hair, the touch sending little shivers across her skin as he went on with his story. ''It's said that in the spring of 1858, the Army's ongoing troubles with the Dineh heated up. There were some raids against the People, who responded by raiding one of Major Brooks's hay camps. It wasn't much of a raid, though an Army dog was killed with an arrow.

"It was probably just intended as a warning to get away, but Brooks retaliated by rounding up and slaughtering more than sixty head of cattle and horses owned by Navajo head man Mañuelito, who was technically at peace with the Army. He'd been grazing them on his own traditional pasturelands, which the soldiers now told him were theirs, and they wanted the slaughter to serve as a warning to others who thought they could use the Army's land. He sent a group of warriors to the fort to protest the action." Logan paused to gauge her interest.

"Um-hm," Eden said, hoping he'd continue touching her, trying to stay focused on the story in spite of the sensations coursing through her.

"There was an incident," Logan went on, "and a young boy, a slave Major Brooks had brought from the East, was killed by an arrow. The soldiers sent troops to demand that the Dineh give up the murderer of the slave named Jim." He paused again, watching the distress on her face. For the first time, the story had become more compelling than the touch. "That incident escalated into full-scale warfare and the people holed up here. In early September, just about this time of year, Colonel Miles wrote out a formal declaration of war and ordered the Army to march into the canyon."

"Ooh." Eden winced, fully caught up in the tale. "I can imagine how those troops felt, marching into this."

"Apparently they started with a great deal of confidence," Logan continued. "They had a Zuni guide who showed them a path that led down from the battlements up there . . ." He pointed. ". . . to the valley floor, somewhere over there." He indicated a slight break in the wall. "They came in from the top, hoping to break up the People and scatter them in both directions.''

''And did it work?'' Eden asked.

''They planned to reach the canyon floor early in the afternoon, then sweep all the way to Chinle before nightfall, but it took the soldiers so long to negotiate the hazardous footpath down the canyon side, that they had to set up camp in a cornfield here at the bottom almost as soon as they got here.''

He grinned, his eyes twinkling. ''It's said that as they were setting up camp, they watched a Navajo signal fire begin to burn on the escarpments above them, then another, and another. By the time it was dark, the cliffs were alive with hundreds of signal fires. The next morning, the troops were up at first light, packing up the whole camp and hightailing it back to Forth Defiance as fast as they could go.''

Eden was enthralled by both the story and Logan's knowledge in telling it. But she knew the ultimate end of the tale had not been happy for Logan's people. ''How long did the wars go on?''

''Pretty much forever,'' he said casually, then, to show her he wasn't being flippant, he added, ''As the Dineh tell it, they'd been at war first with the Spanish, then with New Mexican irregulars and slave traders for a good two hundred or two hundred fifty years before the American military got involved.''

Eden felt overwhelmed by such numbers. ''Two hundred fifty years?''

''Um-hm.''

''That's a long time to fight.''

''For the People, it soon ceased to be a war and became a way of life. Many generations lived and died without ever knowing a period of more than a few short years one could call peace.'' He spoke for a while longer about the tragic events.

Eden had never heard any of these facts in her basic history classes. "I had no idea."

"Most people don't." Logan seemed ready to drop the subject.

Eden wasn't quite ready to drop it yet. "Logan, you spoke about raids against the *rancherías*. Are you referring to places like this one?"

They had climbed out of the riverbed and were looking up now at a small outpost silhouetted against the dun rock wall a half-mile beyond. It was a simple place with an eight-sided hogan of logs and earth at its center, a couple of corrals made of stacked and wired branches, and an out-building that probably served as an animal shelter or corn crib. Eden shuddered to think of how a family might withstand the assault of armed cavalry, with nothing more than this to protect them.

Logan stopped the truck. "Much like this," he said, "though in the earlier days, there were *ricos*, or rich men—like Mañuelito or Ganado Mucho—who had much pastureland and great herds."

"Ganado Mucho. Doesn't that mean Many Cattle in Spanish?"

"You speak Spanish?" He seemed surprised—and pleased.

She smiled. *"Asi-asi,"* she answered, tipping her hand back and forth in the expression that means "so-so."

"Well, you got his name right, anyway," Logan responded. "It does mean Many Cattle. Many of the early Navajos had Spanish names because of their long dealings with the Spanish, and as I said, many of them were quite wealthy, including most of the head men—"

"Is that like a chief?"

"Somewhat," he answered, "although the Dineh followed those whom they trusted, depending on the situation, and most didn't do much following at all. In fact, that's the point I was just making. The People tended to live scattered abroad in small family groups, with little contact with others except during ceremonial times. Their traditional way of life contributed toward making them easy targets of the slave raiders." He shrugged. "Then again, it made it tougher for an outside power to conquer them," he said, gesturing at the canyon around them. "When's the last time you saw a Navajo city?"

Eden considered. "Chinle?" she asked tentatively. If this was a trick question, she hoped her answer was at least close.

"Nope. That city, like most of those on the rez, was created by the European men who came later as a way of organizing governmental activities and trading areas."

"Okay, I'll bite. Which Navajo cities are traditional?"

He smiled knowingly. "There aren't any. Unlike the Kisani," he said, using the Navajo word for their Pueblo neighbors, "the People didn't enjoy living close to their neighbors. It was our style to live in separate family units, each in its own hogan surrounded by acres, sometimes miles, of cornfields and pastures. We never grouped together as others did, except for ceremonies. It made us easier targets for small raids, but—"

"—but safer against large military conquests," Eden finished, recognizing how difficult it would be for an army to round up thousands of people, one small family at a time.

"Exactly," he answered, apparently proud of his pupil. "Between the scattered nature of their dwellings and the natural fortress of this canyon maze, our Old Ones held out for a very long time.''

Eden read the sadness in his voice, recognized the sorrow in Logan's quiet acceptance of his ancestors' eventual defeat, even while she heard his pride in their achievement. ''I'm sorry,'' she said, commiserating.

Something shifted in the mood between them. She felt it instantly, even before Logan's eyes snapped up, pinning her with their gaze. Eden wriggled under his stare, like an insect pinned to a cork board. ''*Why* are you sorry?'' he asked.

She stammered. ''For th-the conquest, the loss.''

''What was your role in it, Eden? Did you wield a rifle? Send your husband out to buy you new slaves for your kitchen? Send your young men out to slaughter our stock where they grazed in the fields, hoping we'd all starve to death over the winter?''

Eden stammered, not knowing whether to feel hurt or angry. ''I—Of course not,'' she choked.

''Then don't apologize!''

Eden felt her spine stiffen. ''I . . . I wasn't. It was meant to be . . . sympathy.''

''Sympathy? What makes you think I need your sympathy?''

Eden bristled. She didn't know what she'd done to start this, but she didn't like it one bit. She stiffened her backbone and fixed him with a stare as icy as his own. ''I didn't say you needed my sympathy,'' she answered, her voice as sharp as his. ''I offered it out of friendship, Logan.'' She tempered her next words. ''Listen, I've obviously touched a nerve here. I didn't mean to. Maybe we should start back now.''

Logan's face darkened, then paled. He stared at her, then

choked out a rough apology. ''I . . . I'm sorry, Eden. I guess I've had my fill of bleeding hearts who want to take personal responsibility for everything that ever happened to my ancestors, then use that as an excuse to make me into some kind of project—or the object of their pity. It was wrong of me to assume—'' He stopped, tongue-tied. ''Sorry,'' he said again, finishing lamely.

His sincerity cooled Eden's own pique. ''I can understand that,'' she said quietly. She'd often felt like more of a project than a daughter to her father—at least since her mother's death. Before that, she meant nothing to her father. ''Pity can be a terrible burden to bear.''

When have you ever experienced pity? he thought, barely able to keep himself from speaking it aloud. *You, the beautiful woman who has had her way paved through life. When have you ever been told to smile and be thankful for the trucks full of other people's hand-me-downs with broken zippers and holes in the knees? When have you and your buddies been herded like sheep into a tent full of people with clipboards, jeans bagging around your ankles while some white-suited physician spent two minutes poking and prodding, then handed you over to another white suit who'd hit you with five different needles before she walked away? When have you eaten week-old bread and moldy cheese under the smug gaze of overfed government workers?* He thought all those things, but what came out was, ''You seem to know something of pity.''

Eden, prepared for a sharp response, was uncertain how to respond. ''I suppose it comes in all forms,'' she said, planning to let the subject drop. Then she realized he expected her to share as he had, and she prepared to tell him a little of her life.

Chapter Five

"My mother died when I was in high school," she began, still not sure how much she wanted to say. "My father was never very . . . very warm or involved in our lives. My high school counselor referred me to a social worker when I took Robbie—he's my little brother—to class with me one day. He'd had chicken pox, but the scabs were healing, and I'd already missed all the school I thought I could afford to miss, staying home with him, so I took him with me."

"Where was your father?" Logan asked.

"That was what the counselor wanted to know." Eden took a deep breath and blew it out in a sigh. "The truth was, I didn't know. We hadn't seen him in a couple of weeks."

Logan swallowed, feeling her pain. He thought of the child she'd been. Perhaps Eden did know something of pity. Maybe she had even deserved some. "What happened?"

"The social worker was in the process of setting us up in a foster home when Dad showed up and threw a tantrum, demanding they give us back."

"And did they?"

She nodded. "My father could always talk his way out of whatever trouble he got into—with my mother, or later, with the authorities."

Logan nodded, this time with some sympathy of his own. "You weren't close to your father."

"I hardly knew him." She sighed. "I still hardly know him."

Logan continued nodding, but his next words seemed more for himself than for her. "It can be difficult to feel such distance from one's own blood," he said. Eden started to ask what he meant, but he shook himself, as though driving painful thoughts away. "Where is your father now?"

"Southern California. He remarried recently, and moved out there with his new wife."

"Leaving dear little Eden to clean up after him," Logan said, referring to the house he had been painting when they'd been together last.

"Yes, in a way you can say that, but it turns out the house was my mother's only, not in joint possession with my dad, and she left it to Robbie and me. I'm really doing my own work when I'm busy getting the house ready for sale."

"I think you're cleaning up after a lazy father who had never cut you much slack," Logan said. "I suspect you've spent much of your life since your early teens cleaning up his messes in one way or another—"

"Not really, Logan. He just—"

"And making excuses for him in the process," he added, starting the truck's engine. "Come on," he said. "It's time to get some lunch."

Still frustrated over Logan's too-perceptive observations about her relationship with her father, Eden spoke little as they drove away.

They continued driving for a time, commenting to each other on small things they noticed. Eden was amazed at the way the canyon changed. Sometimes the two walls seemed fairly close together. Other times the canyon widened until one wall seemed distant and the other almost out of sight. Sometimes there were several homesteads across the width of the canyon; other times a single *ranchería* seemed to fill the canyon completely, and other times there were no hogans, no people at all. Some of the small farms had suburban-style dwellings of wooden frames and exteriors covered in tar paper and chicken wire, as if readied for stucco that never came, but most homes were the typical eight-sided hogans. Eden found them becoming familiar.

After a while Logan turned in at the dooryard of one small hogan and waited for the homeowner to come out to greet them, then negotiated in Navajo for several ears of native corn that had been roasted in the husk. That settled, he bargained with the Navajo householder—a slim, middle-aged man in jeans and red plaid flannel, his legs bowed from long years in the saddle—for a half-dozen fresh peaches.

Though the bargaining seemed fierce, Eden noticed that they reached an agreement quickly. Then, when the farmer brought his peaches out for inspection before money changed hands, he turned them over to her, silently acknowledging her as Logan's companion. It was a heady feeling, almost as if Logan's people—personified in this one man—had opened their arms to take her in. She wondered if Logan had noticed, and whether he'd say anything. Warming under the man's gaze, Eden thanked him profusely as she accepted the proffered fruit.

"These peaches are beautiful," she said to Logan as they drove away. "I've never seen anything like them."

"You're probably used to the peaches in the grocery store," Logan answered. "They're always picked a little green so they won't spoil on the way to the store. These ripen on the tree. The family picks them at the peak of their flavor." He nodded toward the fruit she held. "This is a late-ripening variety, so the peaches we bought just now were probably picked late yesterday, or even this morning. They should be some of the best you've eaten."

"They're certainly among the biggest I've ever seen," Eden said, as she turned a softball-sized fruit in her hand. "And the reddest! I didn't even realize there were fruit trees up here—let alone trees that grew fruit like this."

"You didn't think we had fruit trees?"

Logan's voice held an unusual hint of something. Eden couldn't tell whether the underlying tone was humor or offense. "I guess I just didn't think about it," she answered quickly. "Everything I've ever seen of reservation lands always seemed so barren and dry. I know there's never enough water anywhere in northeastern Arizona, so I guess I just assumed there wouldn't be enough water to grow fruit orchards up here, either."

"In most cases, there isn't," Logan acknowledged. "The rez is always painfully short of water, and most areas are pitifully dry, but because of the streams that flow through the canyon, there's water here all year long, and the families who keep homes here take full advantage of that. The canyon hosts many fruits orchards, and there used to be many more,'' Logan said. ''In fact, in the days before the Long Walk, the People prided themselves on the peach orchards of Canyon de Chelly. Some of those orchards had been carefully tended for more than five hundred years— old stock replaced by new over the generations, mothers handing down the orchards to their daughters who passed them along to their daughters throughout half a millennium. In fact there were more than eight thousand peach trees in this canyon then.''

''Eight thousand?'' Eden mused, once again feeling staggered by the size of the numbers. She looked at the wide, flat fields in the canyon's bottom and imagined them filled with peach orchards, all in blossom. The canyon must have been something to see in those days! ''What happened?'' she asked.

''Kit Carson happened.'' Logan's voice was flat, without emotion.

''Not *the* Kit Carson, the famous explorer who helped to open the West?''

''One and the same,'' Logan answered. ''Colonel Christopher 'Kit' Carson—but whether he 'opened the West' or not may be up to some debate. From the point of view of my people, the West was plenty open before he showed up and brought the blue-coated pony soldiers with him.''

''I suppose that's true.'' Eden hadn't realized she was walking into a verbal minefield, but now that she knew she was in one, she determined to watch her step. ''I always thought he worked farther east, like Texas and New Mexico.''

''He did, to begin with. He had a big career as an Army scout, got a more literate friend to help him write up his adventures, then quit. By the time the Confederacy split from the Union and the United States went to war against itself, Carson was comfortably retired from active military service and working as the government's Indian Agent for the Utes up in the Utah Territory. Then in 1861, when the war in the East broke out, he reenlisted, expecting to be sent back East to fight for the Union.'' Logan paused meaningfully. ''I've often wondered if he would have bothered to sign up again, if he'd known he was going to be sent down here to put down 'the Navajo uprisings.' I rather doubt he would have.''

Once again, Eden was surprised by the tone of his voice. ''You sound like you feel sorry for him.''

Logan considered that for a moment. ''In a way, I suppose I do. He had been a friend of many of the native people he encountered. He even married a native woman and had children with her. Among my people, he had earned the name Rope Thrower, and a reputation as a caring, honest man.'' Logan sighed. ''I'm sure he signed up expecting to be sent to the East. I know he didn't want to get stuck rounding up 'wild Navajos.' ''

Logan looked up at Eden and grinned broadly, one of those quick smiles she had learned to expect when he was about to make a joke at his own—or his people's—expense. ''Unfortunately for us,'' he said, ''Carson went all-out on any job he was asked to do. When he was given the task of rounding up the Dineh for transport to a prison camp in eastern New Mexico, he decided to do it right.'' He looked very sad as he added, ''The man who had been among our greatest friends became our greatest enemy.''

Logan pulled the truck up beneath a spreading sycamore. There was a small, neat patch of grass there, alongside the stream. ''I thought this would be a good place for lunch,'' he said as he set the parking brake and turned off the engine.

"Looks great," Eden answered, lumbering out of the high cab of the truck. As they spread a blanket on the shady grass beneath the tree, she asked, "Tell me about Kit Carson and the peach trees."

"It's not a lunchtime story," Logan warned.

"That's okay. I have a strong stomach."

"Well, all right then. But remember I warned you." Logan set out the roasted ears of corn, the fresh peaches beside them, then offered her a seat beside him on the blanket. He handed her a canteen, took a long drink from a matching one he kept for himself, then began talking again.

"The Utes and the Dineh were traditional enemies. I suppose we had been fighting each other since we both came to this area centuries ago. Anyway, that made the Utes, and the Utes' agent, well qualified to work for the Army in bringing the People to heel. By then, the war Colonel Miles had declared was well into its third year and he hadn't succeeded in rounding up more than a couple of hundred men. When he did capture a few, they just slipped away again and disappeared back into the canyon. I expected it was fairly frustrating for the colonel."

Eden tried to keep a straight face. "I expect it was."

"The Utes weren't afraid of the canyon, and neither was Carson. From the outset of his involvement against the Dineh, he warned the Army that the Navajo nation would not fall until our canyon hideaways had all been routed. He started his campaign with a march through the canyon, he and his troops coming in from one end, a second command marching in from the opposite direction, intending to meet in the middle."

"Was he chased away by signal fires?" Eden husked an ear of roasted corn as she listened.

"He knew better, and he prepared his command to know better. Besides," Logan paused, "by then even the weather had turned against us. During the growing season, the Army harried the People so they were scarcely able to plant a crop anywhere; during the winter, the cold was so severe, it challenged their survival. The Dineh weren't able to mount an army under such adverse conditions. About the best they could do was run and hide, then keep running and hiding."

He paused, looking up the canyon. "The only reason that first march through the canyons was unsuccessful was Carson didn't really know where he was. I guess he was in good company. Columbus was lost when he found us, too."

Eden chuckled. "I guess that's true."

"You bet it is. He only called us Indians because he thought he was in the Indies. The poor fellow died without ever figuring it out."

"You sound like you feel sorry for him, too."

"In a way, I guess I do, though what his adventures did to the indigenous people of Hispaniola is one of the great shames of history."

"Of course you're right," Eden said, then, trying to get the subject back of Kit Carson and his assault up the canyon, she added an exaggerated "Anyway . . ."

"Anyway," Logan went on. "It turned out the group Carson had sent to come in from the opposite side and meet him halfway was actually in a connecting fork of the canyon, the part we call Cañon del Muerto. The two groups never connected because they passed each other unseen."

"Cañon del Muerto," Eden repeated. "Canyon of the Dead?"

Logan nodded. "It's a fork that splits off to the east not far from here. I can take you up that way on another trip, if you'd like."

"And will you tell me why they call it that?"

"If you're certain you want to hear it. It's another unhappy story," Logan warned.

"I'd assumed so," Eden answered, and husked another roasting ear.

"Making a long story short," Logan continued, following her lead to shuck another ear of corn, "that first attack didn't amount to much, but Carson was undeterred. He decided the only way to force the Navajos to surrender was to starve them out, then to be sure it worked, he'd burn them out, too, so they had nothing to return to."

"Like Sherman's march to the sea," Eden said with a shudder.

"If anything, Carson was more thorough." Logan added his shucked ear to Eden's two and began stripping another. "Whenever his men overtook a *ranchería,* they burned it to the ground—all the buildings, outbuildings, corrals, all the fields and crops and personal possessions, all the pasturelands and orchards. Then they topped it off by slaughtering the livestock and leaving the carcasses to rot in the sun. In most cases, the soldiers weren't even allowed to eat the meat of slaughtered Dineh animals."

No wonder Logan had warned her this was not a lunchtime story, Eden thought.

"Would you like me to stop so we can eat?" he asked with a look of sympathy.

"No, it's okay," she said. "I want to hear the rest, and I have a hunch the end is not far off."

"No, not far," he answered, peeling the last of the roasting ears. "Carson knew that the People's heart was in Dinehtah, and that this canyon was the heart of the homeland. He continued his campaign of burning, driving the People ahead of him, while the soldiers in Fort Defiance and elsewhere offered food as an incentive for surrender. In time, some of the People began surrendering to the forts, just so their innocents—their children and old ones—could be fed, but the holdouts kept running into the canyons to hide." He paused, then took a deep breath. His look seemed far away when he continued.

"The winter of 1864 was the coldest ever recorded. At Fort Defiance, near the mouth of the canyon, the mercury fell to almost forty degrees below zero."

Eden gasped. "I can't imagine that! I don't think I've ever seen it fall much below zero, even in the coldest winters."

"It hasn't ever gone below minus ten in my lifetime," Logan answered, "and that only once, but that one winter, all nature seemed to side with the Army and against the Dineh. By then most of the People had been marched to Bosque Redondo and only a few hundred were holed up in the canyon, but the fields and the orchards were still here." Sorrow tinged his voice.

"By then, Carson had discovered his earlier mistake. He began at one end of the canyon and worked his way through, torching everything as he went, and particularly targeting the peach orchards. He knew that if they were gone, the Dineh would have nothing to return to." Again he paused. Eden could hear the pain in his voice, as if he spoke from his own memory. "It's said that between January 15 and 17 of 1864, he burned more than eight thousand peach trees—"

"All of them!"

"—pretty much wiped out everything left in the canyon, and rounded up almost all the final holdouts, marching them all off to their prison camp in New Mexico."

"That's what your people call the Long Walk, isn't it?"

He nodded. "More than four hundred miles with little water and poor provisions, and when they got there, they found the Army's promises of food were well intentioned, but poorly provided. The Army was fighting a huge war in the East—"

"You mean, the American Civil War?"

"Right, and didn't have the means to support a war against the southern rebels and feed the Dineh, too. The People were starving in Bosque Redondo—as well as dying of cholera and smallpox and such. The Army records show that of the first party of four hundred to reach the camp, one hundred twenty-six died within the first week. It was a terrible time." Again his eyes seemed to drift to sights Eden could not see, almost as if he remembered them, though they had taken place more than a century before.

Still moved by the horrible waste of that old war, Eden asked, "Logan?"

"Hmm?"

"If the people were all removed to eastern New Mexico, how do they come to be here now?"

He smiled, another of those sardonic smiles that turned on himself. "Perhaps we have the Southern rebels to thank for that," he said. "It became too expensive to continue to support the Dineh in a prison camp. The early designers of the camp had planned on turning all the People into share-croppers, but they hadn't counted on the sour water of the Rio Pecos. Every attempt at farming failed miserably, and the People depended heavily on stores sent from the East.

Children and old people were dying of malnutrition and disease, infant mortality was close to one hundred percent, and the camps at Bosque Redondo were becoming an embarrassment to the War Department.''

''The War Department? I should have thought a civilian agency—''

''You'd think so, wouldn't you? But early on, the BIA refused to have anything to do with the camps. Running the camp at Fort Sumner became the responsibility of the Army. As you might guess, they had their hands full elsewhere. In 1868, the head men of the Dineh negotiated a treaty and went home.''

''After all that, they just went home again?''

''Um-hm.'' He nodded.

''It seems like such a terrible loss.'' Eden shook her head, not wanting to picture it all.

''Of course it was, more even than I've told you. But in the end, we became one of the few native groups to end up settled on our own homeland. Dinehtah, as it now shows up on reservation maps, is much smaller than our original homeland, but it's ours, and we still have the canyon. Our heart is here, and we were able to come back to it.''

Eden looked up at the distant canyon walls with new eyes, understanding better what this magical, mystical place had meant to the people who had once tended their orchards here—and to their descendants. She felt she understood Logan Redhorse better now as well.

''It's beautiful!'' Eden looked at the intricate panoply of light and shadow, color and shade that spread before her, glorious in its intensity. ''You just keep showing me such natural wonders . . .'' They had come to a small hill near the wall of the canyon and Logan had driven up it, giving

Eden more of a bird's-eye vantage point on the canyon's beauty.

He flashed her one of those breathtaking smiles. "Have I told you today how beautiful *you* look?"

If he had intended to embarrass and distract her, he was doing a bang-up job of it. She struggled for composure. "No, I don't believe you have, but you're welcome to, if you'd like."

He laughed. "All right, I will," he said, but there was no humor in either his voice or expression when he spoke again. "You are beautiful, Eden Grant—as beautiful as your name, as beautiful as paradise." He slipped his arm around her, drawing her close.

"Paradise," she whispered, breaking the gaze before the spell of it carried her away. She looked into the pristine beauty of the canyon. "I almost feel as if we're there."

"We are," Logan answered matter-of-factly.

She cocked an eyebrow. "We are?"

"Or at least, it's close. You see, your people and mine have very different legends of paradise."

He had slipped back into his storytelling mode, giving them both a break from the romantic intensity that had been building around them. Eden followed his lead, easing away as she asked, "How is that?"

"Your stories," he said, his voice almost challenging. "They're all of paradise lost." He must have seen her skeptical expression, because he added, "Think about it. Adam and Eve had perfection in the Garden of Eden— you're named for it—then they fell from grace and were cast out of paradise into the world, right?"

"Right," she conceded. "They were cast into a dreary world full of thorns and thistles, a world where they earned their bread by the sweat of their brow. At least that's the story I was told.''

''That isn't the story Navajo children are told,'' he said, his eyes fixed upon the ruins. ''Our children are told of worlds beneath this one where all creatures of the earth lived mixed together in an ignorant and sinful state, content to be both wicked and slothful until the spirit beings became so disgusted, they decided to sweep them away.'' He turned to face her, caught now in the rhythm of his story.

''Windstorms and floods purged that first world until only the strongest and purest beings remained. They sought a way to leave their ruined world behind and finally climbed a sky ladder. Piercing the top of the sky, they climbed through and emerged into a better realm.

''But they were wicked there, too,'' he continued, ''and were punished again, world after world, until finally they emerged into the sunlight. They had found their paradise.''

He turned back to the canyon, gesturing toward it as he spoke. ''The place of emergence is not far from here. It is shown to every Navajo boy and girl upon initiation into the tribe—and no,'' he added, ''don't ask to see it. Even if I was sure I could find it, which I'm not, I can't take you there.''

''Because I'm *belagaana*,'' she said, making the explanation for him.

''Because you are uninitiated,'' he clarified. ''So you see,'' he said, finishing the tale, ''our legends are of paradise found—and we found it here, in Dinehtah.''

She nodded soberly, letting the realization sink in. ''That explains why your people are so attached to this place.''

''It explains more than that,'' he said. ''Don't you see? Our old ones teach us to cherish this place of our emergence, to treat it with honor and dignity. But if your people

believe they're in a dreary world full of thorns and thistles—''

"—then they feel freer about abusing it," she finished
for him, the full impact of his point settling in. "They care
less about polluting the air and water or ravaging the
topsoil."

"Why should they not? They're looking for their paradise somewhere else."

Eden let out a long sigh. "I never realized how much
difference an attitude like that might make."

"There is much power in the legends we tell our children," Logan said thoughtfully.

Our children. Eden heard the words in a far different
context than Logan had spoken them. The thought was too
dangerous to consider. Instead she asked, "Do you plan to
teach your children of the emergence?"

He nodded. "I promised them I would."

"You promised . . . your children?"

"Um-hm." His look had grown serious, searching.
"That was the commitment I spoke of, Eden."

"A commitment to your children," she said, not
understanding.

He took her hands. "Do you know about my people?"

"Do you mean about your mother?"

Logan nodded. "That's part of what I mean. Among the
Dineh, every individual is identified by his people. I told
you that before. I am Logan Redhorse, born to the Tall
House People, born for the Salt People."

"I remember," she said. "Those are your clans, inher-
ited from your grandmother."

"Right," he said. "And I told you what my grandmother
called my mother's people."

"The Surface-of-the-Earth people," Eden began.

"Yes, or the Paradise Lost People," Logan finished.

"Paradise Lost," Eden repeated, understanding more than Logan had said. Logan's *belagaana* mother had certainly lost a paradise she would never know when she had sacrificed this fine son.

"My grandmother has always been great with me," Logan said, his voice far away, "but there were times when I took a ribbing from people who knew I was claiming my father's kinship. One day—I guess I was about fifteen—I had been praying to be worthy of the kinship I claimed. I looked into the heavens and swore to my ancestors that I would never forget the heritage they had given me. Then I looked toward the future and promised my children that they wouldn't have to borrow their relatives as I had. I swore to them they would inherit an honorable heritage of their own from a mother who was a child of the desert, a daughter of Dinehtah."

Eden nodded. "That's why you thought it better if we didn't see each other."

"That's why." He turned her toward him, lifting her chin so she couldn't avoid his eyes. "I like you, Eden Grant. I think I like you too much, and I don't want to forget the promises I've made to my generations, both before and after."

Eden's heart lurched. She understood now why there could be no future for her with Logan Redhorse, but the energy still buzzing about them told her it was too bad, too bad indeed. Feeling she must say something, she chose to respond to the surface of his comment. "You are lucky to know your generations."

"You said that earlier, about the goats," he answered. Then, "Are you interested in genealogy?"

Eden shrugged, deliberately distancing herself. "Only a

little. I have records of my parents' parents and their parents, then I've got a couple of the family lines back a little farther than that. That's part of the reason I never felt any personal guilt when Native American students I knew in college wanted to accuse me of killing the buffalo and driving their people onto reservations, just because my skin is pale.''

She gave him a careful, sidelong glance, but his expression betrayed nothing. She went on. ''I know my father's family came to New England in the early eighteen-hundreds, after it was well settled, and my family stayed there until my dad left to come west in the nineteen sixties. None of them were involved in the westward expansion.''

''And your mother's?'' he asked.

''As for my mother's family . . .'' Eden sighed. ''There are other modern Americans who might have a case against me, since I'm told that some of my mother's ancestors were Georgia plantation owners who held slaves, but other family records show that a great-great-grandfather on my mother's side was a noteworthy abolitionist.'' She smiled, hoping to take the sting out of anything she might have said. ''Somewhere along the line, I decided the only guilt I could handle was what I'd earned for myself. It didn't always make me popular in my American History classes.''

Logan's answering grin was wry. ''I can understand that. Some modern descendants of the First Nations like to spread the guilt around.''

Eden spoke tentatively. ''I was a little surprised when you seemed so angry with me because you thought I was claiming guilt over what happened to your people. Some of the native students I knew at school would have wanted me to assume all the guilt I could muster.''

Logan made a soft huffing sound, but his expression was

gentle when he said, "I guess we each have our own ways of handling past injuries. Mine is to try to keep the *belagaana* out of my hair."

Eden felt the sting. She suppressed any outward show of it, but Logan saw the expression that crossed her face. He blurted, "I didn't mean—"

"It's all right, Logan. I understand."

He took her hand then, and for a moment they stood looking down upon the canyon, then he stepped a little away from her, breaking the warm contact. "I'm sorry, Eden."

"It's all right, Logan, really. I don't blame you if you want to keep my people out of your hair. Your people have certainly suffered enough at the hands of mine."

"For you, Eden, I could choose to make an exception," Logan whispered.

"I think you already have," Eden answered, quietly smiling. "Thank you for bringing me up here."

"It has been my pleasure," he assured her, tenderly kissing her hair.

Chapter Six

"**P**ass the paint, please," Eden said, reaching behind her for the can she expected Logan to hand down to her from his stool.

" 'Fraid you'll have to reach," he answered. Then, when Eden stood to take the can from him, he touched the tip of her nose with a wet-painted finger, smearing it in dusty rose.

"Skunk," she growled at him. "You did that on purpose!"

"You bet I did," he answered, "and you ought to see how cute you look."

"Cute. Right."

It was Wednesday, and they were working in the hall-way, where they had been since early that morning. Logan had arrived shortly after sunup and had awakened Eden by tapping on her window until she couldn't ignore him any longer. He'd brought breakfast, picked up at a nearby fast-food stand, and more painting tools, as well as a half-gallon of fresh-squeezed orange juice. Had it not been for the juice, one of Eden's little weaknesses, she might have been less willing to forgive him another near-sleepless night. She seemed to have had a great deal of trouble sleeping since Logan started coming around.

"The painting is going quickly," Logan observed.

"Yes, thanks to you. So what do you have in mind for this weekend? It must be pretty special for you to put in all this extra effort helping me paint."

"It is. Special, I mean. Really, it's a favor I have to ask."

"A favor, huh?" Eden made an exaggerated grimace. "If it's such a big favor that you have to spend hours at hard labor before you dare ask it, it's probably either illegal or immoral."

"Maybe just uncomfortable," Logan answered, "that is, depending on how you feel about weddings. I understand some people actually like them."

Eden raised one eyebrow. "Weddings?"

"That's right, but only one this weekend. That would be wedding. Singular."

"Smart aleck. It's the Labor Day weekend, right? Who's getting married on Labor Day?"

"Nobody. That is, no one I know." He reached to get a high spot where the dusty rose paint hadn't quite covered the dirty yellow beneath it. "This couple is going to be married on Saturday. You may even remember them. Max Carmody and Lucretia Sherwood?"

She ignored his joke. "Max. That's Meg McAllister's brother, right?"

"Right. He and I kind of got to know each other this summer while he's been out here visiting with his sister."

Eden's comment was wry. "Apparently he got to know somebody else as well."

Logan grinned. "I think you could say that. Cretia works for Meg and her brother-in-law, Kurt. She did the cake for Chris and Sarah's wedding. Maybe you saw her there."

Eden summoned a vague memory of a slim woman with dark hair who had put together the wedding cake in the yard of the McAllister family home, but all her memories of that day were vague—except those having to do with Logan. He and Sarah were the only people from that entire day whom she remembered clearly. "I think maybe I did," she answered. "Besides, Sarah mentioned they were getting married. Seems to be going around, doesn't it?"

"Among certain groups, anyway."

Eden blushed as she recalled Logan's commitment to his generations. There would be no fear of wedding-fever contagion in this quarter. "So, what time's the wedding?"

"Saturday morning. They're being married on the deck of the new home they just bought for their family—that is, his daughter and her two kids. It's here in Rainbow Rock, just the other side of the high school. Max invited me and suggested I bring a date. So, about that favor? Are you willing to sit through a wedding with me?"

"Sure. I'd like that." *If it's at all like the last wedding we shared together, I may not come away with my heart intact, but I guess I can handle that. At least, I hope I can.* "Sure," she repeated, smiling.

"Beautiful day, isn't it?" Logan led Eden into the front rows of the folding chairs set up in the Carmody's new backyard. They were early. Few other guests had began to arrive.

"It is," Eden answered. "It's beautiful. They must have

put in some serious effort to get the yard looking this good this quickly.'' She gazed around her, admiring the rich green lawn and blossoming shrubs and vines.

''I know they worked hard at it,'' Logan answered. ''I came over a couple of evenings myself to help them put new plants in. Max special-ordered a number of them, in order to get mature or nearly mature plants, and they rolled out sod for the whole back lawn.''

''Well, they did a great job,'' Eden repeated. ''if I hadn't known this was all brand new, I'd have had trouble believing it. By the way, it was awfully nice of you to help here, but I guess I shouldn't be surprised, considering the way you've been helping out at my place.''

Logan shrugged. ''It was no big deal,'' he said. ''I promised to come one afternoon next week, too. A group of us will be moving the rest of Cretia's things in while she and Max are honeymooning. They'll be putting her little place on the market right after they get back.''

''Again, that's very nice of you.''

Again he shrugged. ''No big deal.''

Eden asked about Logan's early acquaintance with the McAllister family, and how he had come to know Max, and he talked about the years since he had roomed with Chris at ASU and the couple of times this summer when he had helped Max move a heavy engine or set up chairs for Chris and Sarah's wedding. Mention of that wedding seemed to make them both a bit shy and thoughtful.

For Logan, the memories were exaggerated when the same violist that had played for Chris and Sarah's wedding took her place on the deck that now served as a dais, next to the bower Max had constructed of redwood lattice. Apparently she had done her tuning inside, for she lifted her viola to her chin, struck the bow to the strings, and began playing a delicate melody.

For the next several minutes, the citizens of Rainbow Rock filed in, taking places on either side of the wide aisle. Both Cretia's family and the McAllisters were so widely known, there seemed little point in separating people according to ''groom's party'' or ''bride's party.'' People sat where they felt most comfortable, the rows filling from back to front.

At a few minutes past ten, the violist struck a chord, then paused, and a hush fell over the assembly. As she began a different, slightly slower, melody, Reverend Phelps entered from the house, taking his place beneath the bower. Max Carmody followed him, looking poised and happy in a dark dress suit and crisp white shirt. Then the music changed again, the ''Wedding March,'' and everyone rose to honor the bride.

Logan turned to look over his shoulder, expecting to see Cretia. Instead he saw Cretia's teenaged daughter, Lydia, walking side by side with Max's daughter, Marcie. They wore matching sleeveless dresses in a soft pink-purple shade and moved a bit awkwardly, as though they weren't quite sure what was expected of them. Still they were effervescent with an eagerness and excitement that practically bubbled over, spilling out into the audience. It was clear how they felt about this union, as if it was their own idea. Logan wondered if perhaps it had been.

He watched the two teens making their way up the aisle and was immediately struck by a memory so vivid, it nearly knocked his breath away: Eden entering from the front door onto the porch of the McAllister home, resplendent in billows of storm cloud purple-blue, her midnight hair tumbling down her back in a tangle of curls that begged to be touched. As long as he lived, no matter what separate directions their lives might take, he knew he would always remember Eden as she had looked on that day. He would hold that image forever in his mind and heart, keeping it as a vision of paradise.

Feeling almost inexpressibly tender toward her, he turned and put his arm around Eden. Her wide, summer-blue eyes read his expression and seemed to recognize where his thoughts had turned. She snuggled, allowing him to draw her closer as they watched the girls move past them. Then it was time for Cretia to enter the aisle, her slim figure draped in ivory bridal satin, escorted on the arm of her eleven-year-old son, Danny.

''She's lovely, isn't she?'' Eden whispered, and Logan nodded.

She *was* lovely, as lovely as any bride he'd ever seen. Still, if he surveyed the room, he'd have to call her a close second to the woman who now stood cuddled at his side. Even now, wearing a simple dress in a rich, royal blue with a short hem to emphasize her elegant legs; even with her hair swept back and held in simple combs; even without adequate rest for the last few days—thanks, in part, to him, Eden was still the most beautiful woman in all of northern Arizona, the most beautiful woman he had ever seen. He turned his eyes from the bride and watched Eden instead, gazing at her with a reverence felt deep in the recesses of his soul.

They're married now. Eden heard the thought in her head as the reverend pronounced Max and Cretia husband and wife and invited them to seal their vows with a kiss. *They're married, as couples who love each other and want to be together ought to be married, as Logan and I could be married, if only . . .*

But there seemed little point in "if onlys." What stood between Logan Redhorse and herself was fixed and unchangeable, a vow she could not ask him to rescind. To take back that vow would mean dishonoring his family backward through generations of ancestors, and forward through generations of descendants yet to come.

So why did I have to fall in love with him? As she thought it, she realized it was true. *You've done it, haven't you, Eden girl? After all these years of distancing yourself from men, of fearing them because of the hurt you've seen your father cause your mother, or Sarah's first husband cause her, after all the times you've warned yourself not to fall for a man who didn't want you, you've gone and done it. Why did you have to pick the one man you knew could not commit to you?*

Briefly she wondered if maybe that was part of Logan's allure, if maybe, deep within, her own fear of commitment was so great, she could not feel free to care for any man who *could* make a commitment to her. *If that's true, you'd better find yourself a good therapist and start keeping regular appointments, honey, because you're going to be a lonely, unfulfilled old maid.* The very thought made her shudder.

Logan noticed. "Are you all right?" he whispered as the reverend presented "Max and Cretia Carmody" and the audience applauded and cheered the newlyweds.

She nodded. "Um-hm," she answered weakly, but she didn't feel all right. She felt desperate, despairing, and a little afraid of tomorrow. The day was coming soon when she'd have little excuse to keep her in Rainbow Rock any longer. She would get in her little car then and drive away, leaving Logan to find the woman who would be a suitable mother for his future generations. She shivered, as if with a sudden chill.

"So that's Massacre Cave." Eden sat beside Logan in the cab of the pickup, staring at the small opening partway up the cliffside, her voice hushed with the uneasy reverence usually reserved for cemeteries or funerals. "It seems so small from here."

"The opening is small," he agreed, "but the cave opens up just inside the mouth and stretches back for some distance—or so I'm told."

"You've never been inside?"

"Never." Eden could almost see the shudder pass through him. "The Dineh avoid places of death."

"Of course. I didn't think." Eden remembered hearing stories of how Navajos feared contact with the dead, even to the extent of destroying a hogan when someone died there. She suppressed a sigh of disappointment as she realized she would not be visiting the cave—at least, not today.

They had come up right after the wedding, taking just long enough for Eden to change her clothes and grab a few things for the desert. Throughout their drive they had chatted about the wedding, the few people both of them knew, the softening weather autumn had brought them. Eden had tried not to fall into the despair that had struck so forcefully this morning, when she realized she loved a man who would never make a commitment to her, who would never honor her with a vow like the one Max had made to Lucretia. Now, as she looked up at the clear evidence of the evil that had befallen Logan's people here in an earlier time, she felt the sadness closing in, towering around her like the walls of the desert canyon, the canyon named for the Dineh dead.

"Was this part of Kit Carson's work also?" she asked.

"Oh, no. The bodies of the massacred ones had long since turned to dust before Carson. That's why this stretch of Canyon de Chelly was known as Cañon del Muerto even before he came."

"Then who—?"

"This assault was conducted by a commander in the Spanish militia, a man named Antonio Narbona."

"Narbona? But wasn't that the name of one of the Navajo head men who fought the Army later?"

"You're right, it was." Again he was looking at her with respectful surprise. "Apparently he was named for the enemy who had done so much damage against the People. Though the Dineh hated him, they respected his ability as a warrior and wanted their son to carry that same fierceness."

Eden felt a chill ripple down her spine. She hated to think of a people so steeped in war that they named their children for enemy warriors. "How long ago did this happen?" she asked.

"It was in 1805," Logan answered. "Narbona brought his command against the Dineh and rampaged through the homeland, overcoming the People with superior firepower until he had driven large numbers into the canyon. A group split away from the main arroyo and took refuge here with their wives and children, finally making their last stand inside that cave." He nodded toward the entrance they were both watching. "Narbona knew they had few weapons, mostly bows and arrows, so he simply lined his men up in rows, far enough from the cave to be out of bow range, but near enough to fire into the mouth of the cave. Then they just started firing and kept on firing until all were dead.''

"Oh." Eden swallowed hard, choking down her response. The image was vivid, much too vivid. She feared her stomach would rebel. "How many . . . ?" She paused, pale, unable to finish.

"Over three hundred," Logan answered, his tone flat. "Men, women, children, infants, elderly. No one knows for sure, since no one inside the cave lived to tell of it."

"I can't . . . Oh, Logan." Eden moved closer, needing to give and receive comfort against the horror of that ancient slaughter. "And the bodies were just left there?"

"Given the revulsion the People feel in the presence of one death, a site where more than three hundred of their own had died was a supremely evil place. No one of the Dineh has approached the canyon's mouth since."

"It's awful," Eden answered, suddenly overdosed on the horror. Her stomach tightened and her eyes glazed with tears, yet her voice remained steady as she asked, "Logan, why did you bring me here?"

His brow furrowed. "You said you wanted to see it."

"I know." She shook her head. "I shouldn't have asked. I'd been thinking as we drove up of our last drive into the canyon. My head is full of the sad part of the history of your people. I'm beginning to wonder if you had an ulterior motive in showing me all of this."

"Motive? Eden, I don't—"

"Are you trying to teach me some lesson about the way my people treated yours, Logan? Is that what this is all about?" She looked so hurt, so genuinely sad.

"It's not . . . I didn't . . ." He sighed. Then he asked himself, *Was there some reason why I felt so compelled to bring her here?* "I didn't mean to hurt you, Eden," he said, remembering that he'd said it before, that he seemed to say it too often.

"But you did mean to drive me away." It wasn't a question. It wasn't an accusation, either. She spoke it as fact.

Logan felt condemned. "Look, Eden, I—"

"When you called and said we shouldn't see each other, I agreed. I didn't understand, but I had felt your wariness around me and I didn't wish to make you uncomfortable."

"Eden . . ." He tried to touch her, but she pulled away.

"Please. Let me say this."

He drew back, waiting. He could see the glitter of unshed tears in the corners of her eyes and he felt her sorrow as she struggled to speak honestly. "When you came to see me after you said you didn't want to see me, I welcomed you, though I didn't understand what you were thinking. When you told me about the commitment you had made to your children, I tried to understand, though I still couldn't see why you would keep coming back to me, when you knew you would never make a commitment."

She gasped, and he realized she was on the verge of sobbing. "I don't understand you, Logan. I don't know what you expect of me."

"I—"

"Sometimes I feel so close to you—as if I know your heart, as if I've always known you." Her voice was little more than a whisper now, and this time it was her courage that awed him. "Other times you cut me off so that I can't know or understand you, no matter how much I might want to."

"Eden—"

"Sometimes you hold me with such tenderness. . . ." He knew; he remembered. "Other times you push me away, reminding me I'm not worthy to be the mother of your children.''

Her words stabbed like knives. *Oh kind heavens! Is that what I really said to her? Is that how she heard it?* ''Please, Eden—''

''Logan, there's something powerful between us, something like I've never known before that draws us together whether we like it or not.'' He smiled wryly then. So he hadn't been the only one to be drawn reluctantly into the vortex of that power. ''But I think the forces that are pulling us apart are even stronger. You have your promises to your generations and I have feelings and memories of my own to protect.''

''Eden, I—''

''Logan, I want to go home.''

He sat looking at her, sure he could not have heard her correctly.

''Eden—''

''Please, Logan.'' Her heard the shakiness in her voice. The armor that protected her bravery was cracking. ''Please, take me home.''

''All right,'' he said, helpless to know what else to say. He started the truck and set it toward Rainbow Rock. ''Eden?'' he asked after a moment.

''Umm?'' She was looking out the window. She was crying, trying to hide her tears.

''Eden, I'm taking you home, as you asked, but may I say something, too? Will you listen?''

She made an odd ''umm'' sound again that might have meant either yes or no. He decided to take it for assent and stopped the truck to make it easier to talk to her. She was crying steadily now—softly, almost soundlessly, her pain betrayed only by little gasps between her silent sobs. The sound almost broke his heart.

"Eden? Oh, Eden." He moved into the middle of the seat beside her and drew her into his arms, fearing she might push him away, surprised when she allowed him to comfort her. "Shh, love, shh," he said, stroking her hair, rubbing her back. "I did want to show you something of where my people have come from, but there was no hidden agenda here—at least . . ." He paused, and his voice rang with honest introspection as he added, "At least none that I planned, none I was aware of. I certainly didn't mean to hurt you." He held her away from him, looking into her eyes. "You believe that, don't you, Eden? You believe that I've never meant to hurt you?"

She didn't answer, but her eyes suggested she was willing to try.

"Eden, sweetheart, I may not want to care about you, but I can't help myself, and I'd never forgive myself if I hurt you deliberately. Please, love, tell me you believe me."

She burst into sobs, pressing her face into the crease of his shoulder. He sat holding her, soothing her, whispering sweet endearments he had never meant to say, but which came so naturally to his lips when he held paradise in his arms. Finally she calmed and he pressed her again for an answer. "Please, Eden, tell me you believe me."

Her words tumbled out in a rush. "Oh, Logan, I want to believe you."

"Then that will have to do," he said, his heart relieved even while his mind insisted it wasn't enough. "Thank you, Eden. Thank you for that much." He gathered her against his chest, holding her until her trembling ceased, holding her as if he would never let her go.

Eden was weary Sunday morning and slept in so late, she barely made it to church. She slipped into a pew beside a young family she thought she ought to know, and smiled in greeting just as the prelude concluded and Reverend Phelps stood to welcome everyone. Then what might have been chagrin or embarrassment changed to surprise as, during the first strains of the opening hymn, Logan Redhorse slid in beside her.

"Good morning," she whispered over the congregation's somewhat discordant rendition of "O, Thou Rock of Our Salvation," wiggling over a little to make room for him at the end of the pew.

"*Ya-tah-hey,*" he answered, grinning that wide, warm smile that never failed to clutch somewhere around her middle. "Surprised to see me?"

"Yes, I am." She couldn't help wondering if he had come here just to see her, or . . . Well, she couldn't guess what else would have brought him.

"Surprised to see me in Rainbow Rock, or surprised to see me here?" Logan asked in a whisper, gesturing around them at the small but overfilled church.

"Both, I guess."

"You wore me out yesterday," he said, his eyes twinkling.

"Well, I think there's some question about who wore out whom," she responded, still whispering.

"Maybe, but either way, I decided I was too tired to drive home, so I crashed in Holbrook with friends. As for church . . ." He made again that small, yet sweeping gesture that seemed to encompass not just their surroundings, but the whole concept of church and religion. "It was a mentor of Reverend Phelps who baptized me out on the rez when I was in my teens. I always make a point of coming here if I'm in town on a Sunday.''

''Baptized you?'' The older couple in front of her turned to look and Eden realized she'd spoken louder than she had intended. She felt her face warm in embarrassment as she smiled an apology.

The hymn ended just then and the reverend rose to pray. ''We'll talk later,'' Logan mouthed as he placed the hymnal in the shelf in front of them.

Eden could only nod an answer.

As the service wore on, Logan took her hand and they sat together companionably, looking much like the young couple who sat just down the pew from them—together, smiling often at each other, holding hands—except, of course, that they were taking turns holding their baby and the mother had a toddler at her side. Eden couldn't help noticing both the similarities and differences, wondering . . .

Well, she decided, *I'm probably better off if I don't do too much wondering.* Still, the knowledge that she and Logan shared a faith helped to overcome at least one major barrier to the possibilities that might lie before them. She barely heard the sermon about diversity and appreciating differences and how all human beings were children of the same divine creator.

After the benediction, while the congregation was still milling around and filing out, Chris and Sarah approached them to ask if they'd like to come to the traditional McAllister family dinner and sing-along which they planned to host at their place that afternoon.

Eden was about to answer when Logan said, ''Can we take a rain check on that and come another day? Eden and I have plans.''

She tried to keep the surprise out of her voice as she told Sarah she'd love to come another time. "What plans?" she whispered as Chris and Sarah turned away.

"Sorry," he said, and when he smiled like that, Eden felt certain she'd forgive him anything. "I hadn't had time to ask you about it. I brought a picnic lunch and I was hoping you'd join me."

"Sounds fun," she answered, touched by his thoughtfulness. It was a few minutes later, when they were alone in the cab of Logan's pickup, that she asked, "You said you were baptized in your teens?"

"Um." He nodded, turning the truck toward the hills. "That was one of the first things I did to make my grandmother mad at me. She beat me with a willow switch until I thought I'd never sit down again."

"So why did you do it?" Even as she said it, she was embarrassed she had asked. She knew why he had done it. She felt the answer in his presence.

"Because I believed what the minister taught."

"Yet you're a Navajo, and you continue to practice the ceremonies of the native faith."

"Yes, many of the Dineh are baptized Christians who still find strength in the legends and rituals of the People."

"But I don't understand—"

"I know you don't. Be patient a moment," he answered, gently taking her hand. "I think perhaps I can show you."

Again she nodded, waiting in silence while Logan drove them out of town and into the hills, onto the reservation lands, into Dinehtah. It wasn't long before he stopped the truck atop a knoll and came around to open her door. "Come," he said, offering her a hand, "walk with me," and she smiled as she took his hand, thinking she might follow this man anywhere he led.

He did not lead her far. A few yards from the truck, he stopped where the earth fell away beneath their feet. They were looking out over a vast expanse of the Arizona Badlands, the multistriped hills for which the Painted Desert was named spread out below them. "Look," he said, but she couldn't have helped looking. The scene commanded attention, its stark beauty and regal splendor a feast to the senses. After a moment, he asked, "What do you feel?"

"Awe," she answered slowly. "Amazement."

"Do you feel the spirit of this land?"

She paused and, for a moment, closed her eyes. Then she knew she did feel it—through the soles of her feet, through the touch of the desert breeze on her skin, even through the penetrating silence. She nodded assent, barely whispering, "Yes."

"Eden," he spoke, his voice intent, and she opened her eyes, turning to face him. "Eden, the Dineh feel it, too, only our tradition has given it a name. When we feel the peace of the home, we say that *Hasch'ehooghan,* or Hogan god, is there. When we feel the spirit of the land, we say that Talking god is upon the land. When we see the lightning storms forming in the hills, we say the *yei,* the Holy People, are coming to bless us."

He raised a hand and touched her cheek, a touch almost as gentle as the whisper of the breeze against her skin. "As a teenager I heard Reverend Willis teach about the creator of all things and I felt the truth of what he was saying, yet I also knew the traditions of my people were, in many ways, metaphors for the truths the good reverend taught me. There are some ceremonies I no longer attend . . ." He let the sentence trail away, and Eden felt his sadness about the parts of his tradition he had given up. "Still, I find few contradictions between one form of faith and the other."

He moved his hand from her cheek to her waist and drew her close to him. They stood together on the cliff, arms around each other, Eden snuggling close as they looked out over the vast expanse of divine creation and shared in the spirit of the land.

Chapter Seven

Eden stretched her back against the seat of the truck. "Are we there yet?" she asked, mischief in her voice.

"Almost," Logan reassured her.

It was Labor Day, and for the past half-hour, Logan had been driving a narrow, winding trail of hairpin switchbacks and stomach-twisting angles where juniper and piñones towered over the roadway. Now as Eden watched, he brought them onto a flat plateau. All that lay above them here was the endless sky and, maybe a half-mile away, the opposing wall of the canyon.

"We're here," Logan said, setting the emergency brake.

"Ah yes, but where is here?" Eden teased, gesturing at the emptiness surrounding them.

"Come on, I'll show you."

He held out his hand and Eden took it, warmed by his touch. She was becoming more accustomed to the nearly electric jolts of energy that shot between them whenever

Logan was near. She no longer started at his touch; now she was content to bask in its warmth, enjoying it while it lasted, knowing the loss would be devastating.

Logan led the way down a narrow trail. Eden followed until they came to the cliff side. He stopped a safe distance back, then pointed at the base of the opposite cliff. ''Look,'' he ordered gently.

Eden looked. At first all she saw was the towering wall of red and yellow sandstone, then, ''Oh!''

''It is something of a surprise, isn't it?''

''Oh!'' she said again. ''Logan, what is it?''

''White House,'' he answered.

Eden looked out across the valley with its meandering stream lined with tamaracks and mesquite. There, on the canyon's opposing wall, lying partly in the shelter of a natural cave some hundred feet or so above the canyon floor, and partly on the valley floor itself, lay the remains of an ancient pueblo. Carefully shaped rock-and-mud walls formed both tall, rectangular dwellings several stories high, and round ceremonial kivas, sunk deep into the earth. ''Can we go down there?'' Eden asked eagerly.

''We will in a little while,'' Logan answered. He handed her a pair of binoculars. ''I thought you might like this view first. It shows you how well camouflaged these dwellings were in the old days.''

''They certainly were that,'' Eden agreed. Using Logan's binoculars, she studied the ruin. Despite its name, the pueblo wasn't white, but it had once been covered in a pale adobe clay that blended into the surrounding rock walls, effectively hiding the village in plain sight. ''I thought your people didn't live together like this,'' she argued, remembering what he'd told her about the *rancherías* on their first drive into the canyon.

"They didn't. The White House is an Anasazi ruin."

"Anasazi," she mused. "The Old Ones. Then the Anasazi aren't ancestors of the modern Navajo?"

He shook his head. "Their descendants, more than likely, are the Hopi and Tewa and other pueblo peoples of the southwest—"

"The ones you call the Kisani."

He smiled, pleased. "Right. The Kisani are all Shoshonean people, using similar languages and continuing to build in the pueblo styles learned from the Anasazi. Their high-rise pueblos always remind me of inner-city apartment buildings. I've never had any wish to live like that."

Eden twinkled at him, looking mischievous. "You know, when you frown like that, it makes a little crease in your forehead, right here between your eyes." She placed one forefinger on the spot.

She didn't know whether he was more pleased or embarrassed, but Logan responded with a mumbled "Hmph." Then a purposeful intensity came into his face as he reached up and took her hand, still poised above his forehead. Holding her gaze, he gently and carefully kissed each of her fingers in turn before intertwining them with his own. Eden heard the sharp intake of her breath. She tried to steady her pulse.

Logan flashed her one of his breathtaking smiles. "Have I told you today how beautiful you look?"

She remembered how this conversation was supposed to go, how it had gone between them before. "No, I don't believe you have, but you're welcome to, if you like."

He laughed, happy to replay their banter. "All right, I will," he said, but there was no humor in either his voice or expression when he spoke again. "You are beautiful,

Eden—as beautiful as your name, as beautiful as paradise.''
He slipped his arm around her, drawing her close.

"Paradise," she whispered, breaking his gaze before the
spell of it carried her away.

He took her hand then, and for a moment they stood
looking down upon White House, then he stepped a little
away from her, breaking the warm contact. "Let's have
some lunch," he suggested. "Then we can go down to the
canyon floor and have a look at the pueblo up close."

"Sounds good." Eden nodded agreement.

"So if your people aren't Shoshonean or descendants of
the Anasazi, who are your relatives? And how did your
people come to be here?" Eden asked. They were wander-
ing among the ruins, examining the evidence of the Anasazi's advanced building techniques.

"Anthropologists tell us we're Athabascan," Logan answered, "most closely related to the Tlingit people of the
northwest."

"The people who make those beautiful Chilkat
blankets?"

"Right, and the totems. I'm told that Navajo and Tlingit
are enough alike that speakers of the two can talk to each
other—at least a little."

"Like the romance languages? Spanish and Italian?"

"I suppose so," he answered. He dazzled her with a
smile. "I've never tried it myself."

Eden answered his grin, then turned her eyes upward.
"Some of these dwellings seem to go up several stories,"
she observed, looking skyward at the remnants of the logs
that had marked the floor of an upper story, the ceiling of
the lower one.

"Five stories here." Logan pointed upward, counting the levels.

"Amazing," Eden said. The day, together with the days before it, was exhausting her capacity for wonder. If the natural beauties of the canyon and the ruins of the ancient Anasazi weren't enough, there was one very modern local feature who was making quite an impact of his own. She feared her heart would remember it for a long time to come. "How large was this community, Logan?"

"Hard to say, probably a few hundred people. More than eighty rooms have been charted. Some may have been simply for storage or ceremonial purposes, but others could have housed large families. Something around three hundred is probably a reasonable guess."

"Amazing," she said again.

Eden looked up at one towering wall and tried to picture White House as it once had been—busy, bustling, teeming with life. For a moment, the present ruins faded and she could almost see the pueblo as it was then, could almost hear the mothers calling to their children, could almost feel in her own legs the strain of the long climb up log ladders to an upper-story room, or the peace of settling down for sleep at the end of a long, wearying day. This place had been home to generations of people who had never seen grocery stores or video recorders or electricity, had never known the tyranny of clocks, but who had lived and died here—happy and fulfilled in their own way of life. She sighed.

"You okay?" Logan asked.

"Um-hm," she answered, nodding. "It's just that . . . I don't know. It almost sounds silly."

"What's silly?"

Eden hesitated. "It's just that . . . I've always been so

grateful for all my modern conveniences, and felt so sorry for people who didn't have all that I've had. Now, to-day . . ." She paused. "It's the first time I've ever wondered if maybe I missed something by not being born here." She looked up and flushed. "See? I told you it was silly."

"Not at all." He gently cupped her shoulders, turning her toward him. "It's not silly, Eden. It shows the depth of your spirit."

"You think so?"

"I am sure." Emotions played across his face, and though she couldn't decipher everything, she saw tenderness there.

"Does it surprise you that I can feel the peace here?"

"Frankly, yes. At least a little."

Eden nodded. "That's okay. It surprises me, too."

Logan responded by drawing her close, one arm about her shoulders. "There is peace here, isn't there?" he answered, holding her warmly.

"Yes. I think I know why the Anasazi came here, and why your ancestors loved this place."

"For peace," Logan agreed. "For solace of spirit." He alone knew how deeply he struggled with the words, how deeply troubled he found his own spirit. He had promised himself he would let Eden go, would give her up as a willing sacrifice to honor the vows he had made. He alone knew what a desperate sacrifice that would be.

Face it, Redhorse. You love her. He gulped, afraid to acknowledge the truth. *You love her and there's nothing you can do about it.* "Let's look around a little," he said aloud, hoping to shake the odd feeling that had just come over him, but even as they moved forward, he knew it was true. He had known better than to tempt himself with

Eden's company. Now, so quickly, he was in love with a totally unsuitable woman. Letting her go would break his heart.

"Look, there's a bit of pottery," Eden said, reaching to pick up a shard that must once have been part of a water jug. As they continued to walk about the ruins, Eden commented from time to time on things she noticed. What Logan noticed was the character of the things Eden saw—small things that suggested the day-to-day lives of the people who had lived here. He watched and listened, fascinated by her insight, her openness. Until he met Eden, he had never imagined that a *belagaana* could exhibit this kind of warmth and vision about a people so alien to her own. What touched him most was the way she saw them—not as alien, but simply as people, not so different from herself and those she loved.

Loved. Logan was awash in emotion, startled by the depth of his feelings. He had never questioned the attraction he felt; that had been obvious to them both from the moment he first saw her. Though the raw power of it was new to him, the emotion was primal and familiar. He had been attracted to beautiful women before. What startled him was how quickly the rest had come, unbidden and unwanted— the admiration of her intelligence and warmth and essential goodness, the respect for her mind and heart. What startled him even more—scared him, frankly—was the tenderness he often felt when he was near her, the desire to hold her close, to protect her from harm or fear, to share with her. . . .

You love her, Redhorse. He cut off the thought. "Are you ready to go now?"

"Okay, if we must." Eden turned to him with a beaming

smile that almost took his breath away and made his heart do funny little flip-flops in his chest.

You're really in deep, aren't you? he cautioned himself as they walked toward the truck. *You've blown it, buster. Falling in love wasn't part of the plan.* Watching the gentle, entirely feminine way Eden moved in front of him, he wished it could be.

"Oops." Eden's single word interrupted his wayward thoughts as she stopped stock-still in front of him. He had to catch himself to keep from plowing into her, then braced them both by taking hold of her shoulders.

"What's up?"

"We have company," she said, gesturing to the trail ahead.

They were on the steep hillside with only this narrow trail to lead them to the valley floor. Given the nature of the "company" Eden had spotted, it looked like they might be delayed a while. Across their path lay a large rattlesnake, stretched out to most of its four- or five-foot length. Apparently it had been making its way across the trail. Now it turned its pointed head toward them and sat poised with its neck raised, flicking its tongue to taste the air.

"I'm glad you saw it now," Logan said. "Instead of when we stepped on it, I mean." As he spoke, the snake rattled a warning. Startled, he drew Eden back toward him.

"It's all right," she said softly, her voice eerily calm. "We aren't close enough to be a real threat to her. Besides, she doesn't mean to hurt us." Logan felt the movement as the woman before him leaned slightly toward the snake. "Do you, girl?" she asked, her voice a purr. "All you want is to go your own way home, isn't that right?"

His mind a blur, Logan watched in awe as the snake tasted the air again, then dipped its head in a motion peculiarly like a nod. Then, as he watched in wonder, it slowly made its way off their path and out of sight. As it moved, he checked all the signs his father and uncles had taught him to watch for—the shape of its head, the size of its middle. There were no sure ways of knowing—short of picking it up and examining parts of its body that no living snake wanted a human to touch—but indications suggested the creature was indeed female. He felt his mouth go dry as he watched it apparently respond to Eden's suggestion, clearing the way so they might move on.

"I think we can go now," Eden said in a steady voice, as if she hadn't just been the source of some sort of miracle.

Logan stared. "How did you do that?"

"Do what?" Eden had begun to walk along the trail, already past the place where the snake had crossed, though he noticed she carefully stepped over its path. From his memory, he heard his grandmother's voice warning him never to step on the trail of a rattlesnake, lest it follow him home.

"How did you make that snake leave?" he said, his voice filled with wonder.

Eden snorted. "Logan, I didn't *make* her do anything. She didn't want to hurt us. All she wanted to do was go home. We were in her way, too, you know."

"How did you even know that snake was female?"

She shrugged. "Who knows? Maybe it wasn't."

He shook his head. Something had happened here, and he wasn't settling for simple explanations. "You knew," he answered. "What I want to know is how."

She turned and looked him full in the face, her eyes sparkling with mystery. "Logan, I was born in this desert just as you were. This isn't the first time I've walked out on it, and that isn't the first snake I've seen." She sighed, glancing away, her eyes apparently fixed on something distant Logan could not see. "Sometimes I feel in tune with it all," she said simply. "Sometimes I just know." She smiled then, like some kind of desert spirit—a *yei*, or one of the Holy People, come to bless or curse his life—and waltzed down the trail.

As he watched her go, he was struck by a thought so alien, he almost didn't believe he'd thought it, yet it hit both his mind and heart with such power, he knew it was true: Eden Grant was *belagaana*, but she was also a child of the desert, a daughter of Dinehtah. The recognition shook him to his very soul.

The shadows of the rabbit brush and creosote were already lengthening as Logan turned his truck toward Rainbow Rock, but the idea that had struck him as they left the White House ruins was lengthening as well. Unable to get it out of his head, he spoke it aloud. "We aren't too far from my grandmother's hogan. I've been thinking about maybe dropping in on her."

Eden, who had been watching Logan since they left the ruins, was aware that something about him, something between them, had changed. She didn't know what it was, but whatever had happened, it seemed to be drawing them forward, propelling them in a new direction. An odd thought crossed her mind: the feeling they were on a course that fate had somehow charted for them, and their future, whatever it may be, lay down this path.

Eden shuddered. *You're getting weird, girl*, she chided herself. She made an effort to shake off the eerie sense of destiny that hung about them in the cab of the truck.

"Your grandmother?" she asked aloud. "Shouldn't we call ahead to let her know we're coming?"

"Can't," he answered. "She doesn't have a phone, but I expect she'll know anyway."

"How?" Eden squinted, skeptical. "Does she practice some kind of second sight?"

He snorted. "Hardly. But you've heard of the grapevine. I've been on the rez all day. By now, word has probably gotten back to her that I'm near."

"Logan, I really don't like dropping in on people at dinnertime. . . ."

"You're thinking like a *belagaana*," he said, taking her hand. "Things are different here."

"I can't help thinking that way. I *am* a *belagaana*, and, to be truthful, that's part of the reason I'm nervous about dropping in. I doubt if your grandmother will think much of me."

"Eden . . ." Logan paused, understanding her implications and suspecting—no, knowing—she was right. "I promise, if she's not comfortable, with *both* of us, we won't stay." He hesitated, then licked his lips. How could he explain to her the sudden need to bring together these two women, both so important to him? How could he share the needs he felt, when he didn't understand them himself?

Eden saw the look in his eyes and acknowledged the truth: she and Logan Redhorse were walking a path that had already been charted for them, a path they needed to follow. *How can that be?* she asked herself in wonder. *He has his promises to his children.* Yet beneath the questions lay the assurance that sensible or not, her conviction was true.

Prying her eyes away from the man she loved, she turned her gaze to the roadway. They had been traveling for some time now, and their road had become little more than a path, leading them away from the paved road to a smaller, graveled road, then a rutted trail barely wide enough for a single vehicle. "Are we nearing your grandmother's home?" she asked.

"We should be there soon," he answered, coaxing the truck up over a rise and down the other side. They were in a depression that might once have been a water course. On the hill at the other side, now almost a silhouette against the red-and-orange glow of the western sky, sat a small *ranchería*, its eight-sided hogan surrounded by simple corrals and outbuildings. "There," he said. "This is where I grew up."

Eden's *belagaana* eyes saw the poverty, the isolation. The desert child within her saw instead how the small earth-covered home blended into its surroundings, the magnificence of the sunset, the simple beauty of the earth and sky. "It looks like a happy place for a boy," she decided aloud. "I'll bet you spent your days chasing lizards and making patterns in the sand."

"And gathering wood and going for water. There's a small stream on the far side of that hill." With a wry grin, he added, "My grandmother didn't believe in wasting available labor. She usually kept me pretty busy."

"But you loved her for it," Eden answered. "Your admiration is obvious whenever you speak of her."

"She was my whole family," he said simply. "She was everything to me." He stopped the truck in the dooryard and together they waited to be acknowledged.

Eden breathed deeply, trying to calm the fluttering of her stomach. Everything she had heard about Logan's grandmother made her sound like an imposing woman indeed, and one not likely to welcome the presence of a *belagaana*, especially a woman brought here by her treasured and very Dineh grandson. She was still steeling herself to the idea of the coming meeting when a tiny, rounded woman, her long hair white with age and wrapped in a bun, came to the door and motioned them forward. She looked to Logan, who smiled and squeezed her hand in reassurance, then she opened the door of the pickup, curiosity almost overcoming her fear.

I should have known it would be like this. I did know it. I just felt I had to come here, anyway. Logan sat on the rugs that covered the floor of his grandmother's hogan, listening as the old woman kept up a steady stream of Navajo, all of it filled with condemnation for Eden's people and, both directly and by implication, for Eden herself.

"Why did you bring her here?" the old woman was saying now. "You know better than to bring a *belagaana* here. Don't you remember what happened to your father when he took up with a *belagaana* woman? How can you even think of bringing such a woman to my home after what that one did to you?" Ella Begay Redhorse, known in an earlier time as Left-Handed Woman, barely stopped to catch her breath as she unleashed an invective of angry, pain-filled words, all of them tying Eden to "that one" who had been his mother.

Logan looked warily at Eden, wondering how much she was aware of. Though the words were foreign to her, it would have been difficult to mistake his grandmother's tone and the disgusted, sidelong glances she kept turning to the lovely woman he had brought here, largely against her will.

Just as Logan had predicted, his grandmother had heard earlier that day of Logan's arrival on the reservation with a woman at his side. The man from whom he and Eden had purchased their lunch had spoken with a friend who was on his way to the feed store in Chinle, who had happened to mention it to one of the clerks there, and thus the story had been passed from one person to another until a neighbor had stopped by the Redhorse hogan to bring a letter from the general store and, after reading and translating the letter for the old woman, had mentioned in passing the news about Logan and the woman. She had prepared extra beans and fry bread, and had added a dish of fresh green beans and yellow squash, fried up in a little bacon fat, in case her grandson found his way home that day. Apparently, that was not all she had prepared.

"I did not take the trouble to raise you in the Dineh way just to have you give yourself up to the *belagaana*," she went on, apparently not the least concerned whether Eden understood her or not. "You have been taught to be one of us, one of the People. I can't imagine why you would choose to behave so foolishly."

" 'Ama-sani,'" Logan addressed her in Navajo, determined to try to calm the old woman, or at least to postpone her angry tirade until Eden would not have to be subjected to it. "This woman is a friend of my friend. I have brought her here to learn something of how our people live."

"You have brought her here to laugh at us," his grandmother answered, firmly setting her jaw, her look and her tone slicing at Eden even while she offered more food with her hands. "You may not see her laughing, but she will return to her friends among the Surface-of-the-Earth People laughing behind her hand at the things she has seen here today, and at the foolish man who brought her to see it. She will go away from Dinehtah with nothing but harsh words for a simple, lovesick fool and a weak old woman."

"It is not like that, grandmother," Logan answered, still speaking in his native tongue—the only tongue the old woman allowed herself to hear. "I am not lovesick for this woman." *At least, I hope I'm not.*

"Bah!" His grandmother interrupted with scorn in her voice. "You cannot tell me this lie. I have eyes, haven't I? They may be dim, but they see the look of the lovesick young. What about your obligations to your people, you foolish young one? Do you not remember that you are born of the Dineh, and that it is among your own people that you will find your companion?"

"I remember, Grandmother," Logan answered, casting Eden a look of abject apology. "I have not forgotten all you taught me."

"I should hope you have not," his grandmother answered. Without excusing herself, she stood and left them, clearing away their plates though neither Logan nor Eden had finished eating.

"Ask if I can help with cleanup," Eden whispered softly. Logan could tell from her expression that she was working hard to be both brave and civil, despite the ordeal his grandmother was putting them through.

"I don't believe that would be wise," he whispered in answer. "I think we'd better go."

Eden nodded—Logan thought she looked enormously relieved—and he rose and went to where his grandmother worked beside a small wood-burning stove, touching her shoulder in a gesture of affection. "I thank you for preparing our food, Grandmother," he said. "And I am glad you are looking well."

"Go," Ella Redhorse answered, barely meeting his eyes. "Take your *belagaana* woman home so she can start her laughing."

"I will visit you again soon," Logan said, trying to hide his feelings. He couldn't help feeling bemused by his grandmother's vision of how Eden must see them all. It certainly didn't square with the Eden he was coming to know. Clearly his grandmother's view of the *belagaana* had colored her relationships with any and all of them, not allowing her to see individuals for who they were.

But I can't condemn her too harshly, he thought guiltily. *I was like that, too, until I met Chris.* As he thought about it now, he was surprised how much his views had changed in the days since he had come to know Chris McAllister. Chris had helped him to learn to trust the *belagaana*, at least some of the time, and it was Chris's mother, Kate McAllister, then later the pretty red-haired veterinarian who had now become Chris's wife, who had taught him that some *belagaana* women could be trusted as well.

With a silent thanks to his friend, he said good-bye to his grandmother and took Eden's arm, preparing to lead her away, but Eden was not quite ready to leave. "Goodbye, Mrs. Redhorse," she said with a slight bow of her head and a studied, finishing-school politeness. "Thank you for a lovely dinner."

"Tell that silly creature I will not let her speak to me," Ella Redhorse answered in her native tongue, casting Eden a look so foul that Logan knew she couldn't possibly miss its intention.

"She says you're welcome," Logan said to Eden.

Eden snapped her eyes in a look that left no doubt as to just how much she believed that, and Logan had to fight the urge to smile. He was also fighting the impulse to tell his grandmother just how ill-mannered she was being. Only the assurance that she would blame his comments on Eden's influence kept him from speaking.

Eden, too, kept her peace. Logan had started the pickup and was turning it onto the rutted trail when Eden leaned toward him with a look of patient amusement. "You're frowning again," she observed, gently touching the furrowed space between his eyebrows.

It may have been the simple release from the tension he felt, but Logan smiled. Then he laughed aloud, barely able to contain his relief and delight. "You are a good person, Eden Grant. It's not everyone who can bear my grandmother's scorn with such patience."

"I didn't want to be patient," Eden answered honestly, looking back over her shoulder to assure herself the Redhorse hogan was no longer in sight. "But I know she is just trying to protect someone she loves very much. That's a motive I can understand, Logan. She doesn't want to see you hurt."

Her eyes shone with a depth of understanding and suddenly, Logan felt a need to come clean. "You know she didn't say 'you're welcome' there at the end," he confided.

Eden answered wryly, "I gathered that. She didn't have a good word to say about me from the time we arrived. In fact, I had the feeling she'd been rehearsing all day."

"I suspect you're right."

"She's wrong about one thing, though," Eden continued. "I won't be laughing behind my hand at you when I go back among my friends this evening."

"*What?*" Logan's mouth dropped open. He swerved off the rutted trail, then brought the truck to a stop and set the brake. "How did you know that?" he demanded. "I thought you didn't speak Navajo."

Eden seemed nonplused. "Oh, I don't," she answered airily. "I doubt I ever could. Aside from *yah-ta-hey* and a few native place names, I don't have a word of Navajo."

"Then how—?"

"It wasn't difficult to catch her drift, Logan. If looks

could kill, I'd be nothing more than a *chindi* by now.'' Logan couldn't help noticing that she had used the Navajo word for ''ghost.''

''But that isn't the same as—''

''Maybe not,'' Eden answered, anticipating the question even before he had finished it. ''But when she put her hand over her mouth and started miming the way a scornful woman sometimes laughs at others, I understood her well enough, Navajo or no Navajo.''

''I see,'' Logan said. He could remember that his grandmother had indeed mimed that action, so the answer made some sense, but he also remembered the way Eden had spoken to the rattlesnake just a few hours before. He wondered if she ''just knew'' Ella Redhorse the same way she had ''just known'' the snake was female, and of peaceful intention. The bitter thought crossed his mind that his grandmother might not be as easily charmed as a rattlesnake.

''It's been a long day,'' he said, confused more by his thoughts than by anything that had happened. ''Come on. Let's get you home.''

Chapter Eight

"I'll be right back with them extra tiles, ma'am."

"Okay, thanks." Eden held the door while the man from the tile store pulled his work kit through.

It was Thursday morning and he had already come once this week, but until today he hadn't carried what he needed to measure the broken tiles she had asked him to replace. Now that he finally had the correct measurements, he said he felt certain his store had those tiles in stock, but he was going to have to go pick up more of them before he could do the job.

Eden sighed as she watched him go. This was just another in a long series of frustrations. She'd spent three busy days on the house since she'd last seen or heard from Logan. After that last horrid scene with his grandmother, she sometimes wondered if she'd ever hear from him again, yet it certainly didn't fit the description of the Logan Redhorse she thought she knew for him to simply abandon her—no visit, no phone call, nothing. So she'd waited and hoped for his call, throwing all her energies into the house.

She'd finished the two smaller bedrooms on Tuesday. On Wednesday the plumber had come to do repairs in the hall bath and on the leaky faucets on the back porch. Eden had spent much of the day in the front yard, and now had that space in pretty good shape. This morning she had painted the hall bath. This afternoon, while the tile man worked, she intended to do a thorough cleaning of the kitchen, getting ready to paint tomorrow. That would leave her with just the master bedroom and bath and some basic cleanup in the backyard. She guessed that by Wednesday next week, Thursday at the latest, she'd be out of excuses for hanging around Rainbow Rock.

"If you're going to see me again, Logan Redhorse, you'd better hurry," she whispered into the quiet of her kitchen.

Just then, the front doorbell rang. Eden checked her watch: thirty-six minutes since the tile guy had left. *That should be just about long enough for him to pick up the missing tiles and get back,* she calculated. She was more than a little surprised when she opened the door to find Logan waiting there.

"Hi," she said, wishing she could think of something clever.

"Hi," he said. "Busy?"

"Well, yeah. The guy from the tile store is due back any second, and I've been working in the kitchen—"

"You look great." His face held that admiring expression she'd seen a few times; it almost took her breath away.

She gulped. "Thanks."

"I was hoping maybe you could get away. There are some people I'd like you to meet."

Eden immediately reached to smooth her hair. ''I'm not in any shape to meet people—''

''Horsefeathers. Like I said, you look great.''

''But really, I—''

''And the tile guy is here now, so you don't need to wait for him. Come on, Eden. Come with me.''

He was right. Eden saw the truck from the tile store pull up behind Logan's and the man get out, walking toward her. She opened her mouth to protest, but couldn't think of any reason why she shouldn't go with Logan. She'd just been commenting to herself on the shortness of the time they had left together, just warning him—however distantly—that if he wanted to see her before she'd left, he'd better hurry it up. *Well, he's here now, isn't he?* she asked herself, and grabbed her purse. She mumbled quick instructions to the tile man, then let Logan offer her a hand as she stepped up into the passenger side of his truck.

''Who are we going to meet?'' Eden asked.

''My family,'' Logan answered. ''That is, my father and his wife, Esther. My sister, Celia, is here, too.''

Eden stared, wide-eyed. ''You have a sister?''

''Remember last Monday when we went to my grandmother's? She had a letter that morning, brought over by a neighbor.''

''I remember,'' Eden answered. *I remember almost every awful minute of our visit with your grandmother.*

''The letter was from my dad. It turns out it's time for Celia's *kinaaldá*—that is, her puberty ceremony—and they want to have it at my grandmother's home. They're in Holbrook to pick up some supplies on their way out to begin the ceremony.''

''Oh.'' Eden didn't know what to say as she prepared to meet the rest of Logan's kin. *I can only hope this goes better than the last meeting with Logan's relatives,* she thought. Aloud, she said, "I'm still amazed you have a sister."

"I expect you'd call her a half-sister," he said as he pulled the truck in next to a battered, older version of itself outside the Kachina Café. "Here we are. They're inside having lunch."

"Great," Eden answered, wishing she felt the least bit of enthusiasm. Not waiting for Logan to come around to her side, Eden opened her own door and swung her legs out. She stiffened her backbone and pasted a pleasant expression on her face as she took Logan's hand then walked beside him, stretching her stride to keep up.

She spotted the Redhorse party as they stepped into the room. Apparently the Redhorses spotted them as quickly.

"Yah-ta-hey." The man who stood to greet them was an older version of Logan—shorter and leaner, to be sure, and a little darker in his complexion, his hair coarse and black instead of Logan's wavy sable. Still, there was no mistaking the resemblance of father and son. They had the same high, prominent cheekbones, the same wide faces and long, patrician noses. Their mouths had the same shape, though she noticed now that Logan's lips were a little fuller. Even their brows were the same—high, wide, and clear—and each of them had a tiny, wayward lock that fell forward regardless of its owner's efforts to comb it back. Eden had never given much thought to what Logan's father must look like, but had she thought about it, she suspected her imagination would have conjured this very man.

Esther, on the other hand, was her image of the typical Navajo woman, only dressed for town, rather than for the reservation, in cotton slacks and a loose overblouse, her hair cut in a fluffy short style rather than bound back in the traditional bun. She wore silver and turquoise in her ears and in a stunning bracelet high on her forearm.

It was Celia who was the surprise. Her long, black hair tucked neatly into a clean French braid, Celia wore her ancestry on her face—a darker, feminine version of Logan's. Yet everything else about her proclaimed her a typical young teen—about fourteen, Eden guessed. From her trendy, high-top sneakers to her blue jeans to her fashion magazine makeup, Celia was a child of her age. The one point in her dress that clearly identified her as native was her T-shirt.

Made of plain white cotton knit, it sported the portraits of four Native American heroes. Eden recognized the one labeled *Red Cloud, Oglala Sioux* and the one labeled *Sitting Bull, Hunkpapa Sioux.* She didn't know the other two portraits, though she immediately knew the name of *Tecumseh, Shawnee.* It was the fourth portrait that caught her attention. Though she had lived on the edge of the Navajo nation her entire life, if it hadn't been for the stories Logan had told her recently, she never would have recognized either the portrait or the name of *Mañuelito, Navajo.* Then as Celia turned to wiggle out of the booth where she'd been sitting, Eden read the legend on the back of her shirt and almost laughed aloud. In large black letters, the shirt proclaimed, *My Heroes Have Always Fought Cowboys.*

"I like your shirt," she ventured, grinning at the girl.

"Thanks," Celia answered, grinning back.

Eden was still smiling as the older man clasped Logan's shoulder in greeting. Then there was a jumble of mixed Navajo and English as everyone talked at once. Somehow, Logan worked into the confusion an opportunity to introduce Eden to everyone, then to introduce "Albert Redhorse, his wife Esther, and their daughter, Celia" to her.

Even in the midst of the confusion, Eden couldn't help but notice that he didn't speak of the man as his father, or acknowledge kinship to either of the women, either. Though that suggested a formal kind of distancing, she didn't feel any tension among the group in front of her. In fact, they seemed very much like family, with a warmth and acceptance she had seldom seen except, perhaps, among the McAllisters.

"They are coming to Grandmother's hogan for Celia's first *kinaaldá*," Logan explained.

"You said that earlier," Eden responded, "but what is a first kin—"

"*Kinaaldá*. My first *kinaaldá*," Celia answered. "It's the puberty ceremony that is held for Dineh girls. I wanted to have mine here so my grandmother can be my . . ." She turned to Logan. "How do you say that in English?"

He tried the word in Navajo, then answered, "I don't know exactly. It means something like 'ideal woman.' "

"Yes," said Celia brightly. "So Grandmother can be my ideal woman." Logan saw Eden's confusion. "There's a woman who leads the *kinaaldá* through her ceremony," he explained. "The girl usually chooses someone a couple of generations older who has been a role model to her for the kind of woman she wants to be as an adult."

"Besides, I wanted a Chinle *kinaaldá*," Celia answered. "They don't do them right in Pinedale."

There followed a flood of spoken Navajo—it seemed to Eden that everyone was talking at once—and through Logan's occasional bits of translation, Eden learned that the *kinaaldá* had once been standard practice among the Dineh, then had become almost passé during the decades of the 70s and 80s. "It's coming back now as more and more young Dineh want to return to their roots," he explained.

"The families sometimes insist on it, too, so their daughters will grow up to be virtuous women, of worth and reputation among the People."

Logan asked in English about singers and through the jumble of both languages that followed, Eden sorted out that Frank Manypersons was to be the chief singer for the planned *kinaaldá*. She knew a "singer" was a medicine man or shaman, one who had spent years learning the songs and chants that encompassed the oral history, myths and traditions of the Dineh, as well as their blessing and curing ceremonies. Other singers were mentioned as participants.

Within minutes, it had been decided when the *kinaaldá* would begin and end, what would be served to the guests, and that Logan—apparently the wealthiest of the honored girl's relatives—would provide the sheep for the feast and the corn for the *'alkaan,* which Logan explained as a kind of pit-baked corn cake that was a traditional part of every ideal *kinaaldá*.

"You will come, won't you, Eden?" Celia spoke as the conversation was breaking up. "At least for the big public day and night?"

"I . . . I don't know," Eden stammered, looking to Logan for help. "Is it . . . can you have a *belagaana* there?"

There was a moment's hesitation and Eden thought Albert and Esther looked decidedly uncomfortable. Then Celia answered, "I can if I want. I'm the *kinaaldá*." She looked to Esther. "Right, Mom?"

Esther answered in Navajo, then seemed to realize she was excluding Eden. She repeated, "That's right, Celia. You are the *kinaaldá*."

"Then you'll come, won't you, Eden?" Celia pressed.

Eden looked to Logan for help, but if he was offering

any, she wasn't seeing it. Finally she answered, "I'll see what I can do."

"Do come," Celia insisted as her mother drew her away.

"I'll see if I can," Eden said again.

Apparently the Redhorses had finished their meal just before Logan and Eden arrived. Now as Albert paid their bill, they started outside to their pickup truck.

"It was good to meet you," Eden said as she nodded first to Albert, then to Esther.

When she turned to Celia, the girl grabbed her hand. "I want you to see what we're all about," Celia said. "Get Logan to bring you out on Tuesday. That's the public day. Come early."

"I'll see," Eden said again, warmed by the girl's eager acceptance. Though neither Albert nor his wife had been rude in the way Logan's grandmother had, she felt a chilly distance in their approach to her.

" 'Bye," she called moments later as she and Logan waved the other pickup on its way toward Ella Redhorse's hogan.

"Shall we get some lunch?" Logan invited.

Eden demurred. "No, thanks. I ate a little while before you arrived."

"Home then?" he asked.

She nodded. "Home."

Logan helped Eden into his truck. Moments later, as they pulled out onto the street, Eden decided to broach the uncomfortable subject. "I suppose you didn't expect Celia to invite me."

"I must admit it surprised me a little."

"I gathered that." Again the silence stretched. "Listen, Logan, I can see what's happening. Your grandmother has no use for me at all, and neither your father nor stepmother is any too crazy about me—''

''They're just not used to meeting *belagaana* in any kind of social setting. They'll warm up.''

''They don't need to,'' she offered. ''I'd only be putting you in a very uncomfortable situation if I came to your sister's ceremony, the . . . what's it called again?''

''*Kinaaldá*,'' he answered, heavily accenting the final syllable.

''If I came to Celia's *kinaaldá*,'' Eden finished. ''So you see, I do understand. Just take me home and we'll tell each other what a lovely morning this has been, then you can make up some excuse about how I was too busy when Celia asks you where I am.''

He gave her a long, searching look. ''Is that what you want?''

She looked away, swallowed hard. ''That's probably what is best.''

''That isn't what I asked.''

Confused, Eden watched the road. They were almost out of Holbrook. Once they reached the highway, it wouldn't take long for them to be back in Rainbow Rock.

''Eden, is that what you want?''

She sighed and faced him again. ''Logan, I'm confused. I don't know what I want.''

''I know what I want,'' he said slowly, his eyes burning with intensity. ''I want to ignore my grandmother's wishes, and pretend I didn't notice my father's coolness toward you. I want to spend this last little while with you before you have to go back to Phoenix.''

His intensity almost took Eden's breath away. ''I . . . I don't know if that's . . .'' she stammered. Then she tried again. "Is it acceptable for someone like me to attend a ceremony?"

He shrugged. "You wouldn't be the first *belagaana* to attend one," he answered. "Besides, Celia's right. She's the *kinaaldá*. If she asks you, it's almost rude for you not to come."

"Celia is the *kinaaldá?*" she asked. "Does that word apply to the girl or the ceremony itself?"

"Both," Logan answered. "It's the name for the ceremony, and for the girl while she is going through the ceremony."

"And it takes several days?"

He nodded. "Um-hm. Usually eight to ten days, though the more open parts last for only the first five."

"And you're coming for all five days?"

"Oh no, I can't get away for that long. I'll come for the fourth day and night, though. As Celia said, that's the public part of the ceremony. They're starting on Saturday, so that will be Tuesday. Eden, will you come with me?"

"You know your grandmother will have a fit, don't you?"

His face was straight, though there was a twinkle in his eye as he answered, "It will be good for her. So, will you come?"

Searching his eyes, she made her choice. "I'd love to," she answered, and watched his face soften in a smile.

"That's it, then." The real estate agent Eden had hired began packing up her papers, including the listing contract Eden had just signed. "We'll put this place on the official home tour for agents on Thursday, and open it to potential buyers this weekend."

"That soon?" Eden felt a sinking sensation. "It's only Monday now."

"We at Babbitt Realty don't let any grass grow under our feet," the woman assured her, tossing her a beaming, hard-sell smile.

"But I may not even be gone by Thursday."

"Oh, no problem. Just tidy up that room you're staying in before you go out for the day. We show lots of homes that are fully occupied. It'll be no problem to work around your few things."

"Oh." Eden tried to smile about the prospect. "Well . . . good."

"You'll be surprised how quickly things can move. You have this place in nice shape, too, so I wouldn't be surprised if it sells fairly quickly."

"That'll be . . . good," Eden answered. Until this moment she hadn't realized it might be difficult to let go of the house she had grown up in, the home where she had known her mother, the place Logan had helped her prepare for sale.

She sighed as she showed the agent out. " 'Bye. Thanks again."

"No problem!" the woman answered, so cheerily it made Eden's teeth ache.

No problem. Her home, and it could be nothing more than a scrap of paper in her file box in a matter of weeks—days, if Liz Corbin had her way. Feeling desultory sadness, Eden wandered through the empty house, remembering. . . .

The rooms were filled with memories: the time Robbie spilled grape soda on the living room carpet and they'd both scrubbed like charwomen to keep it from showing when their dad got home; the day the neighbor's cat had slipped in through an open window to give birth to five kittens in the bottom of Eden's closet; the overnights she'd had in her room with Sarah; the time her mother had taught her to bake snickerdoodles in their kitchen. Mixed in with all of them were recent memories of Logan Redhorse.

He had spent almost all day Saturday with her, despite commitments to his family, already involved in Celia's *kinaaldá*. They had finished the painting together—some touch-up in the kitchen and on the back porch, plus fresh paint in the master bath—and had even taken some time to work in the backyard for a while, Logan pruning the trees and shrubbery while Eden ran the mower. He had been a lighthearted companion, a willing worker, and a steady friend. She didn't want to think about how much she would miss him.

But what if he could have overcome those commitments to his generations? she found herself wondering. *What about your own fears of commitment? If he came to you as a free man, would you welcome him? Or would you find some excuse to distance yourself from him, the way you always have?*

"I don't know," she answered aloud. "How can I know when it's not possible?"

You know, her little voice answered within her.

She looked at her watch and sighed. *He'll be here in just a few hours*, she thought, her heart picking up speed. *We'll spend tomorrow at Celia's ceremony, and after that . . .*

After that, they had no plans to see each other again. She'd load up her little car and drive back to her business and her Phoenix apartment, and Logan would find the woman of his dreams, the one who would become the mother of his already honored children. The thought made her long to sit right down and cry.

The alarm went off at 2:30 Tuesday morning and Eden groaned and rolled over, certain she must have set it wrong. *But it seems like I barely went to sleep,* she thought, noting the time and realizing she was right.

Fighting to open her eyes, she remembered why she was getting up at this horrific hour and argued herself awake. She showered, dressed quickly, did her hair and makeup, then, unable to eat in the middle of the night, she simply waited for Logan.

Remembering how she had felt when she was Celia's age, she wondered if she would not have benefited from having this kind of warm attention as she sat at the dawn of womanhood. That had been a rough time in her life—wasn't it a rough time in any kid's life?—and she couldn't help but feel this kind of caring would have done worlds of good.

Just how much caring, she really had no idea, but she began to realize an hour and a half later as she and Logan pulled into the dooryard of Ella's hogan and had to hunt to find space to park. She counted more than thirty trucks and cars as they walked, hand in hand, toward the hogan.

"Who are all these people?" she asked in hushed tones.

"Relatives, clan members, the singers, and some who came with them." Logan nodded toward a place where a group of children had gathered on the hill. "Guessing from the number of kids here, I'd say we probably have over a hundred people altogether."

"A hundred!" Eden had a hard time imagining where her family would have found a hundred people willing to celebrate with her when she was Celia's age. It astounded her, especially when she realized that many of these people had given up much of this week to share with Celia.

"Come on," Logan said, taking her hand as he ducked

his head to enter the hogan. She entered behind him, her eyes quickly adjusting to the light of a couple of kerosene lanterns. Opposite them, at the western side of the hogan, sat a traditional Navajo blanket.

The space against the west wall, behind the blanket, was empty. To its left sat Celia—looking not at all like the modern teenager Eden remembered, her hair bound up in a bun, her body clothed in a rich red satin skirt and purple velveteen blouse, draped with the most exquisite turquoise squash-blossom necklace Eden had ever seen. Beside Celia sat her grandmother, Ella Begay Redhorse, who barely looked up as Logan and Eden entered, apparently too caught up in her ceremonial role to give the *belagaana* much thought.

At least that's a blessing, Eden thought with relief. To Celia's right, on the other side of the ceremonial blanket, sat a series of three older Navajo men. The most impressively dressed, his white hair bound back with a folded blue bandanna, spoke as they entered and gestured for them to sit.

Taking his place on the floor near the doorway, Logan drew Eden down to sit beside him. ''That's Frank Manypersons, the chief singer,'' he whispered in low tones. ''He says we have arrived just in time. The *kinaaldá* is about to make her dawn run. They'll start the singing then, and there will be no one allowed in or out during the singing.''

Just as he finished speaking, Celia rose and moved quickly toward the doorway where she held back the covering blanket, raised her eyes to the east, and mumbled a few words, then began to run. As she sped into the gathering light, the children who had gathered on the hillside fell in behind her with joyful whoops and shouts.

The singing began then, Frank Manypersons starting

with some simple "vocables." He began on a single pitch
with "*heye, nene, ya-na!*" and the other singers, then the
rest of the spectators, joined in. As they sang, Eden
watched—and counted. She wouldn't have thought the
small hogan was big enough to hold so many people, but,
emptied of its regular contents, it now made room for fifty-
six adults, herself and Logan included, sitting around its
perimeter.

Frank Manypersons led the group in three different ceremonial songs—Logan whispered these were called Hogan
Songs, and they recounted the planning and building of the
hogan of Changing Woman—then there was a brief break,
with much murmuring and quiet talk among the guests,
while they waited for the lookout children to shout that the
kinaaldá was returning. At the shout, Frank Manypersons
began the fourth Hogan Song, timing it so it would end
just as Celia entered.

The song finished and everyone rose. The White Dawn
was thick around them as the party filed out into the dooryard to begin digging the pit for the *'alkaan*. Ella, in her
role as "ideal woman," outlined the circle of the pit in the
earth some thirty yards from her home, then softened the
earth with a pickax. Certain of the watchers began helping
Ella dig. When Eden asked Logan why he didn't help, he
answered he was not permitted to. "Many of us, especially
those who build fires at Squaw Dances and the fire dancers
who carry torches in the Mountain Chant, cannot come near
the fire pit or help with the digging. If we do, the cake may
not cook, but will stay all mushy." He grinned. "Or so my
grandmother thinks."

"Is there any reason why I can't dig?" she asked. When
Logan answered that he couldn't think of one, Eden said,
"Then hand me that shovel," pointing to one a man had

dropped nearby. Logan gave it to her and she began to work beside Ella Redhorse, who gave her an odd look, but said nothing, only motioning to her to stack the free earth on the north side of the firepit. Several other women, and a few of the men, joined them.

The pit was more than three feet deep and almost five feet across when they completed it sometime later. Eden looked at their accomplishment with pride, stretching muscles that seemed to have enjoyed their morning workout, though she had no question they'd be complaining by evening. Albert, in an important though lesser role as the honored girl's father, brought a carpenter's level for the bottom of the pit, then he and Ella fussed with a shovel and hoe until he pronounced the pit was *kehasdon* (Logan translated the word as "straight") and the workers left the firepit.

There followed a period of frenzied activity while some guests harnessed a team of horses to a wagon and went after a load of firewood and others left in a pickup truck with several large drums, heading to the nearby pump station for water.

"Will you be okay if I leave you here for a little while?" Logan asked.

"Sure," Eden answered, despite a sense of unease. "But can I go with you?"

"You might prefer not to," he answered. "It's time to butcher the sheep I bought for today."

Eden blanched. "Thanks for the warning. I'll stay here, thanks."

"Okay, I won't be long." She waved good-bye as he drove away in his pickup with several other men.

Eden watched with the other women while Ella Redhorse used a match to light the tinder in the base of the firepit, then added cedar bark for fragrance. Then she went with the other women into the hogan to change into their finest clothes for the ceremonies to come. Warned by Logan, she had brought with her a floral skirt and clean white blouse, hardly the equivalent of the stunning satins and velvets the Navajo women wore, but more formal than her jeans and plaid shirt. Glad she'd come prepared, she dressed in a sense of companionship with the native women, one or two of whom spoke pleasantly in English, easing away her sense of "otherness."

Some time passed in general preparation before the group sat down to eat breakfast. By then, having been awake for seven hours already, Eden was hungry enough to eat even the lamb and hot herb tea Esther passed to her.

Logan sat next to her, patting her knee. "Good?" he asked.

She nodded, her mouth full. "Mmm," then swallowed. "It's very good. Or maybe I'm just hungry."

"I expect everyone is about now."

"Logan?" They looked up as Esther joined them, acknowledging Eden with a nod. "We're going to need some raisins for the *'alkaan*," she said, and Eden realized she was using English for her sake. "Why don't you take some of the boys with you and make a run up to the trading post?"

"Okay," he answered. "Eden, want to go to the store?"

Esther laid her hand gently on Eden's shoulder. "Maybe your friend would like to stay here for the mixing of the batter. It's about to begin."

Logan looked to Eden. "You might like to see that," he said, "but it's up to you."

Esther smiled. "You will be welcome if you wish to stay," she said.

"I think I'd like to see how you mix the batter," Eden answered, and followed Esther as Logan left again.

She was glad she had, for as it turned out, the mixing of the *alkaan* batter was a spectacle of its own. First Ella spread a clean, white sheet on the floor of the hogan in the west. Then she brought out three large bags of corn meal and emptied them onto the sheet. It was a massive amount of meal, even more impressive when a woman near Eden whispered to her that Celia had ground all this corn herself since the beginning of her *kinaaldá*. What's more, she had ground it using an ancient stone *mano* and *metate*. Eden thought Celia's back must ache even more than her own was beginning to.

Next Ella took a bundle from her medicine chest and knelt beside the meal, facing south and rubbing powder on the *mano*. Rosa, Esther's sister and Celia's aunt, told Eden the powder represented "mirage," or spirit power. Finally Ella added corn pollen from a jar, then handed the *mano* to Celia and ordered her to mix the corn meal from the east, south, west and north. When Celia had done so, Ella told her to work the meal with her hands.

When the mixing was finished, Celia began the ritual of carefully cleaning the *mano*. This began a cleansing ceremony that also included all the jewelry, new and old, belonging to the *kinaaldá*. As Celia began to remove and clean each piece of silver-and-turquoise she wore, Eden drew from the backpack the gift she had purchased for Celia. She whispered to Rosa, "Should I give this to her now?" and Rosa, clearly impressed, nodded. Eden went forward with the heavy silver bracelet in her hands. She presented it to Celia with the words, "A gift for the *kinaaldá*." Celia took the proffered bracelet with a gracious nod, then showed it to the other guests, who all oohed and nodded in appreciation. Even Ella Redhorse gave Eden a more accepting look, and Eden was glad she had thought to make the gift.

It was early afternoon when the men returned from the trading post, and Logan helped some of the older boys carry in a large pot of water that had been set to boil while the group ate breakfast. Some of the guests helped Ella place five large pans near the door of the hogan. On top of three of them were bundles of clean sticks.

"Those are called *'adístsiin*," Logan murmured as he joined Eden among the watchers. In the quiet of the crowd, no one noticed when he grasped her hand and squeezed it intimately. "They are short lengths of greasewood that have been cleaned and stripped of their bark, then tied with damp strips of cloth. Celia will use them as stirring sticks."

Ella brought a pan of boiling water and set it in front of the sheet which held the mixed corn meal. Celia took some of the meal and dropped it in the boiling water, using both hands, then began stirring the mixture with the *'adístsiin*. Another woman brought a second pan of water and Celia began to mix meal into that one as well, then Esther brought in a pan of rich-looking, yellow-brown liquid which Logan identified as white sugar syrup, and a little of this was added to each pan of batter. Then more pans of boiling water were brought in and soon six women were mixing.

More guests arrived, and there was some confusion while the new arrivals and some of the earlier guests took turns eating lunch, more fresh lamb and a few simple vegetable dishes. Eden noted that some women continued the mixing the whole time, replacing one another at the mixing pans. Only Celia and her "ideal woman" never left the mixing. Soon Ella declared the batter mixed and the women began working the now-cooled batter with freshly scrubbed fingers, working out any lumps they might find, while Albert Redhorse cleaned the firepit.

Rosa entered with a kettle of water in which bundles of cornhusks were soaking. "Those husks were saved from last year's corn crop," Logan whispered as Rosa and Esther began the process of straightening cornhusks. Then Ella declared the batter finished and the women left the stirring, allowing the batter to "ferment."

It was then that the women began making ceremonial crosses of the cornhusks. Eden found the process fascinating. Each cross was made of four husks, laid out with the tip of one parallel to the wide end of the other. These were crossed by two others and the intersecting sections were stitched. A second cross was made in the same way.

Much of the day had passed and the shadows were already lengthening when Ella knelt at the north end of the firepit and began preparing it for the *'alkaan*. It was a complicated process involving cleaning out the fire, cleansing the pit and lining it first with paper, then with one of the cornhusk crosses—presented, Logan told Eden, in a "blessing manner"—and finally lining the whole pit with cornhusks.

Eden worked with the other women as they cooperated to carry eleven large pans full of batter to the pit where Frank Manypersons led the men in carefully pouring the batter onto the prepared husks. As the batter overflowed the space created for it, the women added cornhusk, lining up the side of the pit until finally the pouring was completed. Then everyone joined in the happy ritual of adding the raisins onto the corn cake. Finally Ella took the remaining bit of ground meal from her ceremonial basket and blessed the batter, then the women helped her cover the finished *'alkaan* with another layer of cornhusks, finishing it off with the blessing cross.

Over the *'alkaan* and the cornhusk layer, the watchers layered on more paper, then fresh, moist earth and a layer of live coals, topping it all with chips of wood, which immediately burst into flame. With the *'alkaan* now safely cooking, Celia began her evening run, followed by a small crowd of the little children, and a boy from the remaining children was selected to walk to the opposite side of the wash to bring back a four-inch piece of cut ''soapweed,'' or yucca root and some rocks.

Celia and the boy returned at about the same time. A late supper was served and the men filled the *'alkaan* pit with the dirt that remained piled around it. It was well after dark when the men built a bonfire, which Logan told her would be kept burning throughout the night.

''They're getting ready to put the ceremonial blanket over the door of the hogan,'' he said. ''This is the *Bijí*, or special night, so once the singing begins, no one will be allowed to leave. Are you ready to go in?''

''Yes,'' she said, then added, ''Logan, thank you for bringing me.''

''Are you really enjoying this?'' he asked.

She nodded. ''More than I imagined. There's so much warmth here, so much sense of community. And everyone has been so kind. Even your grandmother.''

''I know. She surprised me, too. But I think you really impressed her when you climbed into the pit and started helping.''

''It seemed like the thing to do.'' Eden warned at his approval.

"You certainly impressed me," he said, and the look in his eyes was enigmatic. "Come. Let's go inside for the singing." He took her hand and led her into his grandmother's hogan.

Chapter Nine

Logan sat beside Eden in the crowded hogan, filled with awe. She was singing—in Navajo! She had been singing most of the night. He knew she did not recognize the words she sang, yet she had paid close attention and had learned the syllables of repeating refrains in the various Blessingway songs. Sometimes she whispered quietly to him, asking for translations of the words and ideas, and he did his best in rendering them. Now Eden was participating as fully as most of the Dineh women.

The "special" or *Bijí* night had not really started until the other singers arrived. Then, with the arrival of Freddie Nez and Johnny Bitsilly, the women had served a light meal of mutton, fry bread, and coffee while others brought in small items they would need for the night's ceremonies.

Throughout that long first round of singing, Eden had stayed brightly alert and wide awake beside him, drinking in the details of the eons-old ceremony that surged around them in a combination of modern mirth and ancient solemnity. His mind quelled with awe as he watched her first mouthing, then singing, the sacred words, and his heart swelled with tenderness toward her when the pouch of blessed corn pollen was passed ''in a sacred manner,'' and Eden reverently passed it on, as though she deemed herself unworthy to partake.

Clearly, he had underestimated this *belagaana*.

It had been both a surprise and a delight to him to watch her yesterday as she grabbed a shovel and joined his grandmother in preparing the *'alkaan* pit, and it had been even more satisfying to watch his grandmother's changing attitude.

So occupied in her role as ''ideal woman'' that she had barely looked up when they first came in, Ella Redhorse had turned toward Eden minutes later with a look so full of suspicion and abject disdain that Logan had been grateful Eden's head was turned. Later, when Eden had begun to dig the pit, Ella had jerked around in sharp surprise, and it had amazed Logan that she had said nothing, but had accepted Eden's help. Still later, when it had come time for the first cleansing of the jewelry and Eden had presented Celia with her beautiful and thoughtful gift, Ella had looked toward Eden with grudging respect and approval. Later, as they finished the first round of singing, his grandmother had watched them together, quietly assessing. He wondered what she saw when she looked at them now.

With Frank Manypersons' declaration, *''K'ad ni''* (''It is finished''), Celia had risen and quietly left the hogan, ending the first round of singing so that others were free to rise and move about, or even leave the hogan if they wished. Eden had gone out with the other women. When she had returned a short while later, she was chatting amiably with Esther and her sister, Rosa. That had astonished him almost as much as her digging, and it pleased him more than he could say. He was delighted that she was earning the respect of his family, but their respect had forced him to reassess his own.

What did you expect? he asked himself warily, and he was ashamed for he feared he knew the answer.

He knew his grandmother had been wrong about her. Eden was not like other *belagaanas* who laughed behind their hands at his people. Yet, as he watched his grandmother preparing the soapweed for Celia's final cleansing, he knew he had not really expected much better than his grandmother had. He had not invited Eden to the *kinaaldá* because, in his heart of hearts, he had feared she would be like some he had known who outwardly professed respect for his traditions, then in the same breath spoke of "quaint native ways" or used "primitive" and "civilized" to contrast the customs of his people with their own. Thank goodness for the wisdom of his fourteen-year-old sister who had seen more than he had.

Logan turned his attention to Celia and his heart swelled with pride in the little sister he hardly knew. She was completing the final cleansing ceremony that would make her a fit wife for a man of the People. In an older generation, Celia's marriage would likely have been arranged by the time she reached this point, and he suddenly felt grateful that some of the traditions of his people had changed. It was a blessing that Celia would have time to grow before she took on all the responsibilities of womanhood.

He and Eden joined in for the *Yikai yischií yisin*, "The Song of the Birth of Dawn," while Celia carefully washed her hands and face, then his grandmother rinsed Celia's freshly scrubbed hair with clear water and squeezed it dry, preparing her for the final dawn run.

Thank you, Celia, Logan acknowledged quietly. *Had it not been for your charity, I would never have known Eden as I do now*. He failed to wonder if that was a good thing, or just another way of breaking his heart.

A few of the smaller children, who had fallen asleep during the night's singing, were awakened to run with Celia as she raced into the gathering dawn. While she was gone, some of the women removed the sudsy water and prepared for the day. Ella Redhorse took a place near a small basket and began shaving bits of a piece of white clay into it, preparing for the *dleesh*, or white clay painting. Logan and Eden joined a group of watchers who went to the firepit to uncover the *'alkaan*.

As the guests stood about commenting on the readiness and consistency of the huge corn cake, someone mentioned that the pollen needed to be readied for the next pollen blessing, which would take place when Celia returned.

"Will it be all right if I take the pollen, too?" Eden asked Logan. An expectant hush fell over the group as Logan turned to Frank Manypersons for the answer. The singer paused, appearing to consider, then gave a single, solemn nod, as the group responded with murmurs of general approval.

"Come," Logan told her. "Let's step aside so I can show you how to take the pollen in a sacred manner."

"I've been watching," Eden answered. "I think I can do it."

"Show me," he said, and she did, pantomiming the motions. Again Logan felt his chest fill with pride—and sadness. This woman was so much of what he had looked for, had longed for, yet she could not bridge the past to the future as he had promised his generations. He still had to let her go, only now he knew it would be like amputating a part of himself to send this lovely woman away.

"Yes, you have it right," he whispered, barely containing the emotion in his voice. *Oh, Eden, my paradise, you have so much of it right.*

The watchers called out that the runners were returning and the guests reassembled in the hogan for more singing and the final pollen blessing. Logan could not remember a blessing that had held such meaning for him. His hands shook slightly as he held the pouch for Eden. He remembered his grandmother once telling him that any ceremony meant more when you conducted it for one whom you loved. *And I love her*, he acknowledged, if only to himself, as he watched her take the pollen in a sacred manner and pass it on to bless the next of the guests.

When the singing and blessing were concluded, the watchers all filed outside to the firepit where the corn cake was swept off with a broom of greasewood twigs, then cut by Celia and her mother and grandmother according to a prescribed pattern, a long strip being taken off the eastern side and cut into portions, then distributed among the crowd. Then most of the *'alkaan* was left to cool while the group ate a meal of fry bread, corn mush, and the small pieces of *'alkaan* the *kinaaldá* had served them.

During this meal was the only time the old habit of segregating the men and women during feasting was observed, and he felt sadness at their separation when Eden left him to eat with the other women, yet he did not worry about casting the *belagaana* among strangers. Already Rosa and Esther were treating Eden as if she were one of them. He shook his head again in amazement, stunned all over again by how much she seemed like one of the People, almost as if she had been born to his traditions as much as he had.

The meal ended and people began to gather in the hogan. "What now?" Eden asked as she joined him. He had expected wariness, or, after their near-sleepless night, at least weariness, but Eden still looked as fresh as she had the morning before. Her hair draped about her face with an easy, natural swing and her eyes were bright and untouched from their hours of watching vigil. She had never looked lovelier.

Tenderness welled as he took her hand. "It's time for the painting," he answered.

"Ah, the *dleesh*."

"How did you know that?" he asked. He thought of the way she had spoken to the snake at White House and wondered again if this woman had some supernatural power.

"Rosa told me," she answered sensibly, and settled beside him.

Instantly he felt foolish, but even more so when he could not quite banish the sensation that there was something of the otherworld about Eden.

Frank Manypersons started the first of two Combing Songs while Ella began brushing Celia's hair. Then, at the conclusion of the brushing and the requisite singing, Frank began the White Clay Song, the *Dleesh bighiin*. Quietly, Logan whispered translations of some of the words:

"The white clay of old age. With the white clay, she nears you." By the time he had finished the first repetition, Eden was singing with him.

The music changed, and Logan whispered, "Now the child of White Shell Woman, with the white clay she nears you. In the center of the White Shell House, with the white clay she nears you. On the even white shell floor covering, with the white clay she nears you. On the smooth floor covering of soft fabrics, with the white clay she nears you."

With each repeating refrain, Eden sang the words in Navajo as Logan translated them into English. Again there was a change in the music, and Logan continued to translate the words he had long known by heart: "Her white shell shoes, with the white clay she nears you." As Frank sang this, Ella painted Celia on the soles of first her left foot, then her right. "Her white shell leggings, with the white clay she nears you." Then Ella painted Celia's left and right knees.

The ceremony continued as, with each instruction from the singers, Celia was symbolically "painted" with the white clay that represented Changing Woman's transformation into White Shell Woman. Logan quietly continued to translate as Eden sang with the group the refrain, "With the white clay she nears you." Beneath a rumple in the sheepskin on which they sat, he clasped her hand tightly, feeling closer to her than he had ever imagined, feeling she was a part of him.

When Celia had been properly painted, the blessing of the *dleesh* was opened to everyone and many of the watchers stood in line to receive the small white mark on their foreheads, presented in a blessing manner and painted on by the *kinaaldá*. When the line of watchers had been blessed, Frank Manypersons came to the *dleesh* and rubbed his hands in it, then smeared his cheeks and hair. Finally Celia walked around the hogan, painting all the people who had not stood in line. Logan felt himself touched almost to tears as he watched Eden raise her face to receive the *dleesh* blessing.

It was midmorning by now, and with the final solemn ceremony completed, the watchers tumbled outside in a jubilant air of fun and teasing to mold Celia for the final time. A pile of soft blankets was stacked a couple of feet deep, each blanket borrowed from someone special to the *kinaaldá*, then Celia lay down on the stack facedown while her grandmother completed her final formal task, careful pressing Celia's shape into the blankets: first her left foot then her right foot, her left leg then her right leg, and so on to the top of her head. When they came to this part, Celia made a funny face that caused everyone to laugh before she held her breath and let her grandmother press her face into the blankets.

Frank made a final statement, which Logan translated, "This will help her grow to have a nice shape and be pleasant to look upon," and everyone laughed and made remarks that were only slightly rude about Celia's pretty figure and how she would likely grow plumper with age and the birth of children. Some of the comments Logan translated; others, he chose not to repeat. Still others were said in English for Eden's benefit, and he noted that she laughed in delight even when her cheeks colored warmly.

After the molding, Celia returned all the borrowed blankets and other borrowed objects used in the ceremony, then everyone went to the firepit for the final distribution of the finished *'alkaan*. Even with so many to feed, the cake was large enough to provide generous portions for everyone.

"This is delicious," Eden mumbled around bits of the tender corn cake. "I've eaten cornbread all my life, but I've never imagined it sweet like a cake—and with raisins, too."

"You are enjoying it, then?"

"It's splendid! I'm enjoying all of this, Logan."

"I know you are," he answered, and felt again the sharp pain that would come with their separation. He had been right to see how difficult their parting would be, but wrong to compare it to an amputation. No, giving up Eden would be more like trying to cut out his own heart.

"Is it possible I could have a recipe for this?" she asked as they finished their *'alkaan.* "I'd like something I could bake in an oven rather than in an earthen pit, and something designed to feed a crowd somewhat smaller than the Sixth Army, since I rarely have this many people over."

He smiled. "I think Rosa can probably arrange that for you."

"I'd like that."

"I'd like it, too," he answered, knowing that taking her the recipe would give him one more excuse to see Eden before they parted forever. As he watched her saying good-bye to his relatives whom she now counted as friends, he felt again how very painful that parting would be.

"It was wonderful," Eden bubbled, so alive with energy, she barely remembered how little she'd slept.

They were on their way back to Rainbow Rock and Logan found himself dreading each mile of the trip, since each mile took Eden closer to home and their time together closer to an end. "I want each of my daughters to have a *kinaaldá* when the time comes," Logan said, trying again to remind both himself and Eden of the unbridgeable gulf that separated them.

"Then I envy your daughters," Eden answered—her eyes bright, her voice filled with meaning.

The knot that rose in Logan's throat would be difficult, he feared, to swallow down. "Do you mean that?" he forced out.

"Yes, I do," she answered fervently. "So many of our young teens, both boys and girls, fall into a pit of despair where they feel no one cares for them and life has no purpose or meaning. Imagine how it would feel to a girl of that age to have more than a hundred friends and relatives gather to honor her and to sing her into adulthood." She paused and touched his arm as she said, "Logan, I think a *kinaaldá*, or something like it, would solve many of the problems of our younger generation, at least among our girls. With a ceremony like this, every young woman would know how many people love her and want the best for her."

"That's one of the blessings of being Dineh," Logan answered, though the words threatened to catch in his throat. "A child who grows up in a traditional Dineh family always knows there are many family, friends, and clan members who love and care for him. Whatever may happen in his life on and off the rez, he will always know he is loved."

Eden paused, picturing an abandoned little boy who had needed the acceptance of his extended family and friends. "That's a treasure," Eden whispered, then, remembering her own often difficult teen years, she added, "I haven't ever known that kind of caring."

In that instant, Logan wanted more than anything to be the one who could give that love to Eden. *If only . . .*

But there was no point in wishing. No matter what he might wish for, he still had the promises he had made to his generations.

Silently he drove on until he came to Eden's home where he made as little ceremony as he could of their good-byes, promising he would bring her the recipe she wanted sometime tomorrow. Extending the time he spent with Eden at this point would only extend the heartache for them both. *If only . . .* he thought again as he drove away, but this time the thought reshaped itself into another form: *If only I can bear to live without her.*

"So that's it? You're just going to drive back to Phoenix and pretend it never happened?" Sarah looked as aghast as Eden felt.

"I don't see that I have much choice." Eden sighed. "He told me from the beginning that there'd be no future in our relationship, that we'd only have a little time to enjoy each other's company."

"That's ridiculous." Sarah's dander was up, her normally pale complexion reddening as she spoke. "Can't the man see how right you are for each other?"

Eden's voice was resigned as she asked, "Are we, Sarah? I wonder."

"No. Don't tell me you're falling for all that talk about what he's promised his children—children, might I add, who won't even be born unless he finds a mother for them."

"I know. I said the same thing myself, at first. It wasn't until I went with him to Celia's *kinaaldá* that I really began to understand. The Navajo people have a network of strong traditions that have held them together over the centuries, in spite of the Mexican government and the American government, in spite of the Kit Carsons and the wars of conquest and the plagues and—"

"Okay, okay. I don't need a history lesson, for Pete's sake. And you don't need to give up so easily."

Eden couldn't help but smile at the determination she saw in Sarah's face. Over the years, she and her very best friend had always strengthened one another in times of weak resolve, and here Sarah was, willing to fill that role in her life yet again. "You're true blue, you know that?"

"Through and through," Sarah answered, repeating the refrain they had spoken to each other often throughout the years, first as girls, then later as grown women. "And I'm not going to see you throw away the best chance you've ever had at being as happy as I am."

"I appreciate the thought, girl, but—"

"But nothing! Get in there and fight, Eden!" Sarah looked ready to fight dragons, if that's what it took. "You want this man, so go get him!"

"I would, if it were that easy," Eden answered solemnly. "But it's Logan himself I'd have to fight if I decided to go into this battle."

"Don't you love him enough to fight even him, if that's what it takes?"

Eden had asked herself that question many times through the long night that had passed since Logan had left her at her door, hurrying away from her as if pursued by those very dragons. She had answered it, too, in the peace of her own heart. By now she knew that if there was some way, any way, to bring Logan around without destroying him . . .

"Of course I love him, more than even I knew until I had to face giving him up. But fighting this out of him would destroy a large part of what I love most. Don't you see, Sarah? He is what he is partly because of his traditions, and if I force him to give up a part of his loyalty to those traditions, it will crush a large part of the life and passion right out of him. I could have him that way, I think, but he wouldn't be the man I love now, and he'd never be completely happy. I love him too much to see him lose that happiness."

Sarah mumbled something quite unladylike.

"Sarah!"

"I can't help it, Eden. I care too much about you to

watch you suffer like this. And I like Logan, too. I can't help thinking that no matter how much he'd lose by giving up his promise, he'll lose even more if he lets you out of his life.''

"Oh, Sarah, I wish it were that easy."

"There's got to be a way." Sarah began pacing, her face tensed in concentration.

"Please, Sarah. Quit now, before you think of some cockamamie idea that's only going to prolong the agony and make everything worse for both of us. Please?"

Sarah paused, staring long at her friend with that picture of fixed concentration on her face, then reluctantly, she capitulated. "Okay, but if something occurs to me—"

"I'll be the first to know," Eden finished for her.

Sarah grinned. "You've got it, sis."

They hugged, Eden holding on desperately, as if she feared letting go. When they finally separated, both were blinking back tears.

"So you're all loaded up and ready to go?"

Eden nodded. "Um-hm. I'll see Logan one more time this afternoon when he comes to give me his aunt's recipe for the corn cake, then I'll toss my purse in the car and take off for Phoenix."

"Well, one thing you've gotta say." Sarah smiled through her tears. "It's been the most interesting visit you've made back home in a while."

Eden laughed in spite of herself. "There's no kidding about that," she answered. "I'll never forget it. Never, as long as I live."

Sarah grabbed her again for one last good hug. "I just pray that you don't regret it for as long as you live."

"Me, too, honey. Me, too."

The sun set early this late in the autumn, and it was edging toward its rest by the time Logan's truck pulled up in front of Eden's childhood home. Already she had sent the bed she'd slept in and the dresser where she'd kept her few things off to the local thrift shop, loaded the last of her mother's keepsakes into her little car and finished the final cleanup. For the last couple of hours she'd had nothing to do but wait, and fight back tears. As she watched Logan striding up her walk, she feared she'd simply break down the moment she opened the door. She reached it just as he did, opening it while he still had his hand raised to knock. "Hi," she said.

He opened his mouth to speak, then closed it and stepped forward instead, wrapping Eden in an enveloping embrace that said everything he couldn't quite bring himself to say aloud. For several long moments he held her, just held her, as if this simple act could will away the distances and traditions that separated them and bring them the union they desired. Then slowly he let her go. "I . . ." He tried again. "Eden, I . . ."

Eden took pity on him. "I know. I'll miss you, too."

He nodded, then reached into his shirt pocket. "Here. Aunt Rosa's recipe for a small corn cake you can bake in your oven."

Eden's lip trembled in spite of her effort to smile. "Thank you. Thank her for me, too, please."

"I will."

"Logan, I just want to say that . . ."

"Shh, love." He touched a finger to her lips. "Shh, don't say it."

"But I feel I have to. I want you to know that I underst—"

He caught her by the upper arms and kissed her hard,

kissing her into silence. Finally he held her away again. "There's nothing to say," he whispered. "We both know how this part has to go. We've both known all along."

"I just didn't know how difficult it would be," she said.

"I didn't, either." For a moment he looked away and there were tears in his eyes when he looked back. "I love you, Eden. I didn't mean for it to happen, but it did. I love you, and it's breaking my heart to let you go."

"Oh, Logan, do we have to do this? Isn't there a way—"

This time he put his hand over her mouth to stop the words. "Please, love. Please don't say anymore. If I could think of a way of making this right, you know I would. I can't, and I'm sorry. It isn't fair. Loving you isn't fair." He drew away from her. "It isn't fair!" he said again, then he turned and sprinted for his truck.

Not caring if the whole neighborhood heard her, Eden shouted after him, "Logan! Logan Redhorse, I love you, too!"

As he drove into the deepening night, she slumped onto her porch step, quietly sobbing.

The yellow dawn was just catching up with Chris McAllister as he turned his pickup truck toward Many Farms, praying that he'd find a way to help his suffering friend. It had been nearly a month since Logan had driven away from the best thing that had ever happened to him, and Chris had watched him carefully since then, afraid for Logan. He'd never seen his friend so despondent.

Eden was no better. For more than a week now, Sarah had been calling her friend every day, and every day she ended up hanging up the phone and turning to Chris, begging him to find a way to help. "We've got to do something," she had said just this morning after a near-sleepless night of worry. "I've never seen Eden like this. She wasn't even this bad when her mother died."

"I don't know what I can do, but I'll try," he had promised the wife he adored. "I love them both, too, you know."

"I know," Sarah had said, and had held him as if she never wanted to let go. Since he was the kind of person he was, Chris turned his eyes heavenward, acknowledging the silver lining to this cloud. Because of the misery of their friends, he and Sarah had been reminded once again of how blessed they were to have each other.

He pulled into the dooryard of the goat project and spoke to the boy who came out. *"Yah-ta-hey."*

"Yah-tah-hey," the boy answered, raising his chin.

"I'm looking for Logan Redhorse."

"He ain't here."

"Know where he is?"

The boy gave him a long, assessing look. "Who's askin'?"

"I'm Chris McAllister. Logan and I are buddies."

"Yeah, I know. He's told me about you. I'm Philbert." The boy stuck out his hand, and Chris could tell that whatever Logan had said about him had worked. He'd plainly passed muster with Phil. "Logan took a walk out in them hills early this morning. He's been gone awhile now." Though Phil didn't say it, Chris could tell he was worried, too.

"Think I'll hike out and see if I can find him."

The boy nodded. "Shouldn't be too tough," he said. "He's wearin' them big hikin' boots with the waffle soles."

"Got it." Chris tipped his hat to the boy. In the sandy

soil of the foothills near the mouth of Canyon de Chelly, Logan's boots would leave a fairly distinctive track. Chris located, then followed that track, not knowing what he'd say when he found his buddy, but praying that he'd find the words to turn all this sorrow into joy.

Logan sat in the warmth of the yellow morning, his back against sun-warmed sandstone, his eyes closed against the glare of the autumn light, his mind awhirl with all the questions he dared not ask aloud. He had done the right thing, hadn't he? He hardly braved contemplating the possibility that he might have been wrong. This much pain surely had to have a purpose! But if Eden was so wrong for him, why did she seem so right? And why had he been led to her, and so completely drawn to her, if only to send her away? Was he being asked to test his resolve? If that had been the cosmic purpose behind these past few weeks, he hardly wanted to know about it. It was all too big, too painful, too unfair.

He didn't notice the sounds of another climber until a stone rolled on the path just in front of him and he jerked into alertness, snapping his eyes open. "Who's—? Oh, Chris. *Yah-ta-hey*, buddy. Whatcha doin' way out here?"

"Thought I'd come check up on an old buddy of mine. I've heard he's had some hard times lately." Chris brushed off a clean spot on the sandstone and dropped into a squatting position such as Navajo men often took.

"Yeah. Take a number," Logan teased, his eyes not nearly so angry as his words. "Everybody wants to check up on me lately."

"Hey, can you blame us? Ask yourself when's the last time you looked this bad."

Logan chuckled mirthlessly. "Yeah, I do look a bit like something that's been beaten and left for dead."

Chris grinned. "Not quite that good, actually." He paused while Logan snorted, then lowered his voice. "You know, she's not doing any better than you are."

Logan groaned and dropped his head in his hands. "Please, Chris. Don't tell me. I've spent so many sleepless nights worrying about her. I can't forgive myself for what I've done to hurt her, yet I don't know what I could have done differently. I tried staying away from her, but you see how well that worked . . ." He let the thought trail away.

Chris laid his hand gently on Logan's shoulder. "Maybe you couldn't stay away from her because you're not supposed to. Maybe she's the one, Logan."

"Don't you think I want that?" Logan jerked up, throwing Chris's hand off him and jolting into a half-standing position that looked poised for a brawl. "Don't you think I'd have given anything if I thought she could be?"

Chris kept his voice calm. "I don't think you ever seriously considered the possibility."

"How could I?" Logan looked half-mad with pain and guilt. "Chris, you know the promise I made to my generations. You're one of the few I ever told about it. I can't go back on that. I can't! I wouldn't be who I am if I violated that promise."

"And what exactly was that promise, Logan? Say it again. Say it aloud so we can both hear it."

Logan let his eyes drop shut with a heavy sigh. He had repeated these words so many times, both to himself and others. He had no doubt he could say them in his sleep. He probably had, more times than he could count. "I promised them they wouldn't be without heritage as I was. I swore they would inherit an honorable heritage of their own from a mother who is a child of the desert, and a daughter of Dinehtah.''

Chris waited a few pregnant beats before murmuring, ''And who's to say Eden is not that woman?''

''Oh, come on, Chris! You know she's not. She's *belagaana*, not of the People.''

''I didn't hear anything about her having to be Navajo.''

''But you know what I meant.''

''I know what you said.''

''You're trying to confuse me.'' Logan's eyes looked confused, Chris thought. They looked downright bewildered. ''You're just trying to make me think that what I want is what I really need.''

''And why not?'' Chris asked, ever so sensibly. ''Can you find a better mother for your children than someone you love as much as you love Eden?''

''But my promise—''

''What of your promise? You promised the mother of your children would give them an honorable heritage. Granted, Eden's dad isn't much to brag about, but she's an honorable woman from good stock—''

''Just not—''

''Shh. It's my turn. You can give your children a fine, strong heritage with Eden as their mother. You told them you'd marry a desert child. Tell me Eden's not that. You know she is. She was born here on the high desert just as you were, and she loves it just as much as you do.''

Logan nodded, remembering the snake, their day at White House. He had known then that Eden was a child of Dinehtah. ''But that's cheating,'' he said finally. ''It's like changing the rules to fit the circumstances.''

''Why not?'' Chris asked. ''You're the one who made the rules.'' He paused while he drew squiggly lines in the sand with a twig. "You know, Logan. You remind me of a king in one of those silly fairy tales who won't do the right thing for everyone because it would break the law. All along he keeps forgetting that he's the king and he made the law. He can change it if he pleases."

"You're just trying to confuse me," Logan said, but this time there was less passion in it.

"I'm trying to make you see sense. You and Eden are perfect for each other. You have been from the beginning, and in your heart of hearts you've known it. You're afraid to make that commitment to her because you can't help remembering how hurt you were by having a *belagaana* mother who ran out on you. Along the way you've conveniently failed to notice that Eden isn't anything like your mother, that she is loyal to a fault and would never run out on a husband or a child, that she loves this desert as much as you do, that she even loves your traditions. She is the mother you promised your children, Logan, but you're going to lose her if you don't get your head out of the sand."

Chris stopped, afraid he may have gone too far. Logan sat like a wounded thing, curled in on himself, hurting. It took some time before he lifted his head and looked at Chris with pained eyes. "How can I be sure?"

Chris softened as he touched Logan's shoulder. "How can anyone ever be sure?" he asked. "Life is full of risks. But you know what your heart is telling you. There are people you trust, too, people besides me. Go to them. Get their advice. Then you've got to go with what you think is right."

Logan stood, calmer than he'd been in some time. He clasped Chris on the shoulder. "Thanks, buddy. You are a good friend, better perhaps than I deserve."

"You deserve the best," Chris answered. "That's why I want to see you with Eden."

For the first time in nearly a month, Logan smiled. "Maybe I need to think about that," he answered.

Chapter Ten

Logan pulled his pickup truck into the dooryard of his grandmother's hogan. *It looks different,* he thought. *But of course, there was* a kinaaldá *going on last time I came here. That would account for the changes.* He failed to notice that the last time he had come here, he had been with Eden. Eden's presence changed everything.

You know what you're doing, don't you, Redhorse? his little voice niggled as he waited for his grandmother to acknowledge him.

"Yeah," he answered aloud. "I'm doing just what Chris suggested. I'm going to those I trust for advice."

You're going to your grandmother first because you already know what she'll say. She will be grateful you got rid of that belagaana *woman. You won't even have to ask. You're not giving this a fair chance.*

"Since when is anything fair?" he grumbled aloud, afraid to recognize the truth of what he heard.

Ella Redhorse came to her door and motioned him in. Minutes later, he sat at his grandmother's table, sipping strong coffee from a tin cup and listening as the old woman complained of pain in her hip and how the cooler weather affected her joints.

He wondered how he would bring up the subject of Eden, then realized he wouldn't have to. "Where is your pretty *belagaana* friend?" his grandmother asked. "Didn't you feel like bringing her with you today?"

He took a long, slow sip of the rich coffee. "She has gone home to Phoenix," he answered.

Ella made a sound deep in her throat that might have been agreement, or a scoff. "She is a good woman, I think."

Logan dropped his coffee cup, scalding himself with the hot liquid. He grabbed a rag from the sideboard and began wiping up the mess, careless of the small burns on his hands. "I thought you didn't like her," he said after a moment, trying to regain some degree of composure. "I thought you called her 'one who laughs at us behind her hand.' "

"You're right, I did," Ella answered. "When I met her, I thought she was like others I had met. I thought she would be one to tell the sheep how to eat grass." Ella used the phrase Navajos often used for busybodies who stuck their noses into everyone's affairs. "Then I saw her at Celia's *kinaaldá*. I think now that maybe I was wrong."

"You? Wrong?" It was a good thing Logan hadn't poured more coffee yet, because he surely would have spilled it again. In all the years he had lived with Ella Redhorse, he could never remember her admitting to a wrong, even when he'd angrily rubbed her nose in it.

"Yes." Ella nodded her head soberly, as if this choice

required deep reflection. "I think now I was wrong about your Eden friend. She is not of the People, but she is a good woman, and you are a better man when you are with her, my son."

"I—" Logan stopped in mid-sentence, sitting with his mouth open. Of all the things he had imagined his grandmother saying, this was not one of them. Was it possible she was right? Dared he even hope?

"Why did she go to Phoenix?" his grandmother asked after a time.

"She has work there, a home. She owns a business."

"Did she want to go? Or did you send her away?"

Again Logan found himself without words. He had always thought of his grandmother as perceptive, but this! "I guess I sent her," he finally answered, feeling guiltier than ever.

"You were afraid to see she might be right for you."

He stammered, then, unable to find suitable words, he answered, "When did you become so wise?"

"I have always been wise," his grandmother answered. "You just have not always been wise enough to see it."

Logan chuckled as he said a fond good-bye.

"So you've come to me to make up your mind for you." Reverend Phelps stood up from his desk and paced a few steps. "Why me, Logan? And why didn't you just make up your own mind?"

Logan hardly knew how to answer, especially since he wasn't sure of all the answers himself. "I can't say for sure," he answered. "I came to you because I have always been able to trust your advice, and because I knew you wouldn't mislead me, at least never deliberately. As far as making up my own mind goes, I did what I thought was right in the beginning and it only seemed to hurt—not just me, either, but everyone involved. It was Chris McAllister who suggested I ask for advice from people I trusted. He told me I might be making a mistake I would long regret.''

''Does it feel like a mistake?''

Logan nodded. ''So far, yes, it does, but when I choose the woman who will be the mother of my children, I'm making a decision that will affect many unseen generations. Frankly, that terrifies me. If that choice is a mistake, it's one they will all have to live with.''

''That's true,'' the reverend said, drumming his fingers on his desk. Then he turned to Logan. ''You know I can't really advise you on this decision. It's too personal. You are the only one who can make this choice.''

''But I was hoping you'd have some advice, at least.''

''Then again, I might be prejudiced. I like you, Logan, and I like Eden, too. I might just be swayed to suggest what I think is right for the two of you without considering those future generations that have you so concerned.''

Logan waited, suddenly realizing the good reverend was coming to a point.

''What I think I maybe can do is pass on some good advice that was once given to me. The man who told me this was a faithful man, a believer not of our faith, a fellow you'd call *belagaana*. He was also a very wise man indeed. He died some years back, but not before he'd taught me more than I could ever learn in a lifetime on my own. I wish I knew half the great wisdom about people that this fine man might have shared with me.''

Reverend Phelps filled a paper cup at the cooler, then slowly drained it, letting his words so far sink in. ''I went with this man to an ecumenical conference many years ago when I was just beginning my ministry. He was approached by a man who was having trouble with his wife. That man wanted my friend's advice on whether the children should live with him or with his ex-wife, once the couple had separated. My friend gave him a long look, then he said very soberly—and Logan, I've always remembered this. He said, 'The best gift a man can ever give his children is to love their mother.' ''

''Well, the man who'd approached him said, 'No, you don't understand. I don't love their mother anymore. I want to know whether the kids will be better off with me or with her after we separate.' Then my friend gave him a gentle look and said again, 'The best gift a man can ever give his children is to love their mother.' So that's my advice to you too, Logan. Whoever your children are, whatever their tradition, whenever they come, the best gift you will ever give them will be to love their mother.'' The reverend sat again behind his desk. ''So, are you sorry you came?''

Logan didn't feel sorry. He didn't look sorry, either. ''No,'' he said, as his grin grew and widened. ''No, I'm not. In fact, I think that was exactly what I needed to hear. Thank you, reverend.''

''Don't mention it.''

Logan left the church offices feeling lighter and happier than he had in some time. He practically ran up the street toward where he had parked his truck. As he neared the vehicle, he noticed another familiar truck pulling up outside the Kachina and shifted his gait, jogging toward the café.

''Logan,'' Esther said as he approached the family group. ''We didn't expect to find you here.''

''We looked for you out at your place,'' his father said in Navajo as he took his son's hand.

''We've been worried about you,'' added Celia.

"I'm fine. I'm doing just great," Logan said, feeling it for the first time in a month.

"You haven't sounded great when we've talked to you lately," Esther reminded him.

"Not since Eden left town, in fact."

That was like Celia, Logan thought, always saying out loud what her elders only hinted at. "I thought maybe I'd make a trip down to Phoenix," he said, testing the waters. "See if maybe I could have a little visit with Eden."

"See if maybe she'll come back with you?" Celia asked.

"Celia," her mother said, following it with a rapid chiding in Navajo.

Celia didn't seem to mind. "Are you going to ask her to marry you?"

"Celia!" her mother said again, and this time Albert joined Esther in warning Celia that she should not try to teach the sheep how to eat grass.

Logan smiled. "Would you mind if I wanted her to marry me?" he asked the family in general.

Albert looked at Esther and they held the gaze for a moment, then both fired warning looks at Celia, who paid no attention at all as she answered, "I wouldn't mind. I think Eden's really cool."

"Celia," her mother said again, but Celia went on.

"She's not like other *belagaanas,* Logan. You saw the way she acted at my *kinaaldá,* almost as if she is one of us. She's beautiful, and sweet, and I think she's just what you need."

"Celia!" Esther chided, then said to Logan, "your sister has been spoiled, I think. It is not our place to say what choice you will make in this."

"But you wouldn't mind, would you, Esther?" he asked, seeing the approval in her eyes.

"No, I wouldn't mind," Esther answered slowly, "And neither would your father, though it would pain him to say so."

Albert grumbled a few rough words in Navajo, and Esther smiled. "So, Logan. Will you join us for some lunch?"

"Nah. Thanks, Esther, but I don't think so. I have a long drive to make today, and the sooner I get started, the sooner I can get there."

"You wouldn't want to be late," Celia teased, poking at him just a little.

"I fear I may be about a month late already," Logan answered. He heard Celia giggling in the background as he jogged back to his truck.

Eden sighed as she set the phone in its cradle. "That was Geneva," she told Laurel, the bookkeeper and payroll clerk for the Old Woman's Shoe who was already doing double-duty as a backup teacher.

"Is she sick, too?" Laurel answered as she cleared away the remains of the afternoon snack. "She didn't look well when she left here after lunch."

"She took a nap and when she woke up, she was running fever of a hundred and two," Eden answered. "She's calling to let us know she probably won't be able to take her early shift tomorrow."

"I don't know how we'll replace her," Laurel said. "Almost all our backup staff is sick."

"I know," Eden answered miserably. "If we're lucky, some of those who caught this bug early may be almost ready to come back."

Like other businesses that dealt with the public, the Shoe had gone through its share of flu epidemics over the years, but they'd never seen anything this bad. "It's probably a blessing that the children all have it, too," Eden said as she pulled out her backup call list. "If we weren't already down by a third of the kids, we wouldn't have enough staff to stay open."

"We still might not," Laurel said, responding to the ringing telephone.

Eden waited until Laurel had finished. "I hope that wasn't another teacher calling in."

"Nope. It was Mrs. Jarvis," Laurel answered, naming one of the women whose three children were regulars at Eden's day care. "She said the children weren't *very* sick anymore, and asked if we'd still take them in the morning."

Eden grunted. "She knows better than that. We've never taken ill children before, and we can't afford to start now, though the way we're going, half these kids are likely to come down with this bug before the day is over."

"At least that's only a couple more hours," Laurel said, looking at her watch.

"Omigosh," Eden said, noting the time. "Who was supposed to have the curriculum for the last activity time?"

"Miss Dana was working on it yesterday," Laurel answered. "When she called in this morning, she said it was all prepared in the second drawer down in the teacher prep cupboard."

"It was Thanksgiving stuff, right?" Eden asked as she began to dig through the drawer. "Pilgrims and turkeys and such?"

"That's what I remember," Laurel answered.

Eden dug through the drawer, looking for the cutouts Dana had prepared and realizing how her politics had shifted since she'd begun to think more of how her native friends saw the holidays. "Not everyone is quite so thank-

ful for Thanksgiving,'' she mumbled. Then, laying hands
on the file, she realized that, politics or not, she was grateful
for an activity she didn't have to prepare. That would make
this next hour ever so much easier. She grabbed the file of
Pilgrims and turkeys and a bottle of glue, some plain white
construction paper, and crayons for the children to write
their names. ''Come on, everybody! Come to the tables!''
she called as she gathered the playing children around her.

Half an hour later, she was up to her elbows in white
glue and wishing the Pilgrims had worn simpler costumes
when she heard the front door open. *I hope one of the
parents has come early,* she thought idly. Anything to take
the pressure off would be welcome just now.

She stood and turned around, ready to put on a happy
face for the parents who made up her clientele. But it
wasn't a parent.

''Logan, what—?'' She paused in mid-sentence as her
knees turned to jelly beneath her. Her mouth still half-open,
she slumped back into her chair.

''Hi, Eden,'' Logan said. ''Looks like I've caught you
at a busy time.''

''Uh . . . um . . .''

''Yes,'' Laurel answered, protectively stepping in. ''It's
a very busy time. Is there something I can do for you, Mr.,
er . . . ?''

''Redhorse,'' he answered. ''Logan Redhorse.''

Laurel's eyes widened. ''Oh. Redhorse. Oh. You're
the—''

''It's okay, Laurel,'' Eden said, finally finding her voice.
''I'll handle this.''

''Okay. Sure thing, Eden. Can I take over the Pilgrims
and turkeys for you while you two, uh, talk?''

"I'd appreciate that," Eden answered. "Logan, would you like to step into my office?"

"I'd like that," he said, noticing how unsteady Eden was on her feet as he followed her. He shut the door behind her as she stepped into the room. "Are you okay?"

"No," she answered unevenly. She didn't look the least bit happy. "No, I don't think so. What are you doing here, Logan?"

He managed a small smile, an effort to cover his disappointment. *Well, what did you expect, Logan? Did you think she'd throw herself at your feet?* "I've missed you, too," he said, attempting a joke.

Eden didn't smile. "What are you doing here?"

He'd hurt her. He knew he had hurt her. Maybe he hadn't realized how much. "I was joking when I said I'd missed you." He reached out to touch her arm; it was a simple effort to connect. She pulled away, dodging it. "I was joking," he said again, "but I have missed you, Eden. I've missed you terribly."

"Is that all you have to say?" she asked, her face defiant. "Because if it is, I've got three teachers out with the flu and I need to get back to my Pilgrims and turkeys." She turned her back on him.

He took her by the shoulders. She flinched, but allowed the touch. "I'm so sorry I hurt you, Eden. Please believe—"

"What difference does it make?" She turned, her eyes flashing with anger and limpid with tears. "You did what you said you'd do all along, so what's there to apologize for? And why did you come here today if all you're going to do is dredge it all up again?"

"That's not . . . Eden, that's not why I'm here."

She finally looked, really looked, at him. "Then why are you here?"

This would all be so much easier if she'd let me hold her, he thought. "Can we sit?" He gestured toward one of the chairs.

Eden eased into the chair at the desk and he took the other. Then she waited.

"Eden, I've done a lot of thinking," he began.

She nodded. "I guess one *can* do a lot of thinking in a month."

"You're not about to make this any easier for me, are you?"

She took a deep breath. Her voice was gentler when she said, "Okay, I'm listening."

"Eden . . ." He cleared his throat, then started again. "Eden, I was wrong."

She raised an eyebrow. "About what?"

"About the promise I made to my children."

Eden was out of her chair before he finished the final syllable. "No, Logan. I don't want to hear this. Please leave now, before we hurt each other anymore."

"You don't understand." He caught her arm, stopping her movement toward the door. He put all the feeling he could muster into his voice when he spoke again. "I wasn't wrong to make the promise. I just misinterpeted it."

Eden eased back into her seat, and Logan went on. "It took me a while to realize it, some miserable weeks and a quiet talk with Chris, then another with Reverend Phelps, but I know now that you're what I was waiting for all along. You are what I promised them."

Eden blinked. "Me? Logan, you're not making sense. You wanted a Navajo mother for your children, someone who could give them a clan affiliation of their own."

"That's what I thought I wanted, but it was Chris who pointed out to me that it was never what I *said*. I always *said* I wanted my children to have an honorable heritage with a mother who was a child of the desert, and a daughter of Dinehtah. *You* are a child of the desert, Eden. I've known it since that day at White House."

She smiled, looking inward. "Yes, I remember that day."

"My children can have their clan inheritance the same way I do, through my Dineh side. That is, *our* children can. I want you to be their mother, Eden."

"Stop, Logan." She rose again. "I can't have you compromising what you really want just because—"

He didn't wait for her to finish. He caught her arms instead, kissing her with all the force in him, letting her feel how much he meant his words. Perhaps her anger was melting now, because she kissed him, too. In fact, her response gave him the first hope he had felt since he'd come here today. He released her only briefly, holding her close against his chest, kissing her mouth and eyes and hair as he whispered over and over again, "Oh, Eden, Eden. I've missed you so much. I don't know how I'd live my life without you. You are what I've always wanted. You, only you."

Finally believing enough to let her go just a little, he held her at arm's length, watching her eyes. "I love you, Eden. I think I've loved you since the first moment I saw you walk onto Chris's porch. You fascinated me long before I knew anything about you, and the more I learned, the more I wanted you near me."

"Eden, I want to spend my life with you, to love you and cherish you and keep you close beside me forever. I want my daughters to choose you as their 'ideal woman,' and my sons to grow up honoring your name. Marry me, Eden. Marry me and be the mother of my generations.''

Eden felt stunned, shocked, as though her world had just shifted beneath her. "But what about your children?'' she asked. "What about your promises to your children?''

"*Our* children, Eden. Yours and mine. I don't even want to have children if you aren't their mother.''

"But—''

He kissed her quiet. "Don't argue, love. Not now. Just tell me you'll marry me.''

Eden took a long, deep breath. The confusion seemed to clear away with the fresh air. "All right, Logan. I'll give you an answer. But first, look me straight in the eyes and promise me that if I accept your proposal, you won't ever regret being married to a *belagaana*.''

Logan smiled. "That one's easy.'' He held her directly in front of him, hands on her shoulders, as he said, "Eden Grant, I love you with all my mind, life, and heart. I could easily regret marrying just any old *belagaana* woman, but I could never, would never, *will* never regret marrying you—never for all of my days or all my generations.''

Logan saw the life come back into Eden's face. He saw the smile begin from the inside out, spread first through her eyes, then to her mouth, and finally even into her voice. "I do believe you mean that,'' she answered.

"I do. I swear I mean it. Marry me, Eden. Say you will.''

"I—''

A sudden pounding on the office door interrupted them. "Miss Eden! Miss Eden!'' a young voice called. "Miss Eden, Timmy's eating the paste again.''

Eden felt her lip quiver. "You mean you really expect me to give up all *this?*''

Logan grinned. "Promise you'll marry me, and I'll deal with Jimmy."

"Mr. Redhorse, you drive a hard bargain."

"Then it's a deal?"

"I love you, Logan. I've spent the last month wishing I'd never met you because I've been so miserable without you."

"But does that mean yes?"

"Yes! I love you, Logan Redhorse."

"I love you, Eden," he said, and took paradise in his arms.